GREATNESS
REVISITED

MATT PRIDGEN

**LIONHEARTS
PRESS**

lionheartspress.com

GREATNESS REVISITED

Copyright © 2020 by Matt Pridgen

PUBLISHED BY LIONHEARTS PRESS
www.lionheartspress.com

Cover art by Juliet Crews

ISBN 978-0-9854127-6-0

Printed in the United States of America
First Edition 2020

GREATNESS

REVISITED

To my wife, Nicole,
for never giving up on me

and

To our men and women
in uniform across the globe,
thank you for your service

BOOK I

I

Make America Great Again. The hat vendor at the mouth of the terminal had been more aggressive than suited Jim's taste, but he needed a cap and thought it strange that this was the only one the man had available at his kiosk. The hat *was* red, and red *was* his favorite color as a boy growing up, but he thought now that there was no place for nostalgic sentiments any longer in a work-a-day world. *Diversify your portfolio, man,* he thought with a cross between a smirk and a sneer on his lips, *and you will do better for yourself and for your family, if you have one.*

Jim needed a hat to cover his face, not for shame, but for sheer practicality, to avoid recognition as much as possible which is tricky business in your home airport, in your home-town, in your home district. He had left his wide-brimmed Stetson at home and had already kicked himself half a dozen times for the oversight on the taxi ride over to catch his flight. "What's done is done," he caught himself speaking out loud and then closed his mouth promptly to avoid attracting any negative attention.

The terminal pulsed with activity, from midweek business travelers meticulously following the arteries and veins of their prescribed and predictable courses to the early summer vacationers who sauntered to and fro, horizontally rather than vertically, attempting to restrain their children's erratic and hyper-energized movements, each one holding the potential to throw the entire rhythm of the corridor into chaos. Jim looked on as the two forces awkwardly collided—a business traveler halting abruptly for a darting child, pausing for a moment with a blank expression that radiated utter disdain at the momentary loss of efficiency. Then seconds later, the showdown was over and both parties each went on their way again, the child back to its mother's side for a comforting embrace and the business traveler on to his gate to conquer the world.

Just then, Jim's phone buzzed. He shimmied in his seat just enough to extract the device from his front left jean pocket and wiggled what he always thought to be an oversized appliance out into the open air. *Remember when cell phones were actually phones,* he reminisced as he pulled his reading glasses out of his shirt pocket and balanced them squarely on his nose. He knew the thought itself dated him, but he didn't care. In the quiet moments between the hustle and the bustle of his endless days, he longed for simpler times.

He knew before he even looked at the text that it was his mistress. He had everyone else on "Do Not Disturb," including his office and even his own wife and children—especially his own wife and children. Being a native Peruvian, her broken English always made him chuckle.

"I am waiting for you, mi amor, for kisses and love. My heart is heavy for you, why do you delay? I watch your flight, no more delays, you are arriving here soon please."

His heart raced. Something about her tone always sent his libido soaring over the moon, in person especially, but even over text her word choice always seemed to make him lose his mind a little bit. It was the reason why he was willing to put everything on hold—to put life on hold—to see her. For just a few short days. It was worth it. He needed this. He needed some romance in his life. *All work and no play makes Jim a dull boy,* he thought as he keyed in a much more grammatically correct response.

"Second flight delayed two hours, plane here now and should be boarding shortly. I long to be in your arms and to hold you in mine, mi amor."

Normally all this texting stuff got Jim in a frazzle. "Just pick up the phone," he would say to his aides regularly, "and we'll have the whole thing sorted out in two minutes!" But on this occasion, he liked the back and forth of the text conversion—the tug of the dramatic pause, waiting and longing for a reciprocating response to close the feedback loop, the vulnerability of airing his heart, the little love notes like Cupid's arrows piercing one another and making each other love sick. It had been a long time since he had fallen head over heels in love.

It's a human necessity, Jim justified to himself. *One would die if they went too long without love.*

II

Jim slipped his phone back into his pocket, and as he glanced up to check on the status of his flight, he noticed something peculiar out of the corner of his eye. He turned his head toward the center aisle which ran the length of the terminal, and what he saw there caused him to jump to his feet before he even had a moment to think. Less than 15 feet in front of him stood a massive American bison which must have weighed a literal ton. His heart began pounding in his chest, and his mind raced like a Derby winner on the home stretch. His lungs felt like they were going to explode as he tried to cry out, but he could not make a sound.

The great beast stared straight into his eyes with its enormous brown head swaying gently from side to side and its two white horns pointing straight up to the ceiling. Jim stood paralyzed, unable to believe his eyes and wondering why no one else around him even looked remotely concerned about the two thousand pound animal capable of trampling them to death at any moment.

He had smoked some peyote in his college years, and although it did not exactly cause him to hallucinate, it certainly blurred the lines between reality and fantasy in his mind. Ultimately, the stuff did not sit well with him and he had never tried it again, but the memory came racing back at this moment like a freight train and he wondered if he was having some sort of flashback. The one similarity which made him seriously consider this conclusion was that the world itself and all of reality seemed to grind to a halt, and a deafening silence roared through his consciousness as if he and the creature, both mammoth and majestic at the same time, were the only two beings in all of existence.

Although his rational mind told him to run as fast as he could in the other direction, Jim found his feet carrying him slowly but surely, one cautious step at a time, toward the giant animal which he had grown up affectionately calling a buffalo. When he traveled out West as a child, they were a dime a dozen as they graciously roamed the plains of the national parks his family delighted to visit. But even only a few decades later, the scarcity of the species alarmed him and made him cherish his childhood memories of their carefree grazing all the more.

As he reminisced, something continued to draw him to the great beast like a magnet, and his mind did not have the power nor the wherewithal to resist. Before he knew it, he stood nose to nose with the bison separated only by about two arms lengths, and time itself seemed to stand still.

"Jim," the massive animal spoke with such gentle firmness that everything inside of his being quaked from top to bottom. "I have been waiting for you."

Although he could hear the voice audibly, he did not perceive that the words were coming from the beast's mouth, but rather from its mind directly into his.

"How, what—what on earth is going on here?" Jim felt like the mighty creature could read his thoughts, but he spoke in his normal voice all the same, almost for his own benefit simply because he did not know how to put substance to his thought process otherwise.

"Jim," the great bison continued, "you and I have had an appointment scheduled for quite some time, and now is that time."

"Who, who are you?" Jim managed to eke out, still trying to find his poise and regain control of his frozen vocal chords.

"I am Tatanka, and to you, right now, I represent the spirit of the Native American people."

Jim's mind raced back to his childhood days. He had never known anyone personally of Native American descent, so the pictures that flooded his mind were of textbook drawings, Pilgrim and Indian plays, museum exhibits, old Westerns, and more recently, flamboyantly dressed activists who occasionally graced the halls of the State House with their tireless persistence and passionate concerns over traditions he knew and cared nothing about.

"Why are you—why am *I* here?" Jim said a bit more calmly this time. His nerves remained on edge, but his heart rate, although noticeably still elevated, was beginning to level out.

"The Great Spirit has sent me to you," Tatanka replied evenly and deliberately, "to question you about matters of justice. You are a chief, are you not, a ruler of your people—or as you say, a legislator?"

"I am," Jim said with an abrupt exhale, almost as a sigh, never for a moment lowering his gaze from the burning eyes of the colossal animal. "But wait, are you real? Is this a dream? What is happening to me?"

"I am a spirit animal, Jim," continued Tatanka. "You are fully awake, and this is not a dream. I am real in the sense in which you mean it, that is, I have materialized in your world. But I am far more real than that."

The burning eyes of the enormous bison seemed to peer into

the depths of Jim's soul, and he could do nothing at the moment but simply return the gaze with unbroken engrossment.

"If there are no more questions, I would like to continue," Tatanka picked back up gently. "What can you tell me about Manifest Destiny?"

Again, Jim's thoughts returned to his grade school days as sudden regret seized him for the quantity, and quality, of naps he took in Mr. Robertson's 10th grade Honors US History class.

"I believe," Jim began cautiously, swallowing hard to clear the lump in his throat, "that those who championed Manifest Destiny—" Jim's voice sputtered out as he averted his gaze to the ground and started rubbing the back of his neck with his hand. "Hold on a second. What does this have to do with justice or my being a—what did you call it—a chief? I know my history, and I don't need to be questioned by you or by anyone else about it. What are you angling at here anyway?"

"Jim," the massive bison spoke after a brief pause with great patience in its voice, "you must understand that I am here for your good. I want nothing from you but your cooperation. There are some things I must show you, but you have to be willing to trust me and to trust this process. This has everything to do with justice and your role as a legislator, but you have to work with me if you are going to receive anything from our encounter."

Jim put his hands on his hips and slowly rocked back and forth for a few moments, as he was prone to do while engaged in deep thought. He remained silent for the better part of a minute and then finally spoke up.

"Ok," he said emphatically, clapping his hands together as if he had made up his mind. "It's not every day you run into a talking buffalo, so hey, you've got my full attention."

"Alright, let's begin again. Tell me, what do you know about Manifest Destiny, Jim?"

Jim scratched his chin for just a moment and then picked up where he left off before. "I believe the folks who championed Manifest Destiny considered it our duty, our divine call from God to occupy America, the continental United States, from sea to shining sea." He paused for a moment and then added an additional thought that suddenly came to his mind, "And I suppose conversely, that anyone who got in our way was therefore opposing God and his divine plan for our nation."

"And what did happen to those who stood in your way?" Tatanka asked without skipping a beat.

"Well, you would have to look at it case by case," Jim said thoughtfully, "but for the most part, they were either killed or displaced—bloody massacres, endless warfare, the Trail of Tears—driven further and further West, until there was nowhere left for them to go."

"Yes, and do you believe that that was the end of Manifest Destiny?" Tatanka continued with his line of questioning. "California and nowhere left for them to go?"

Jim reflected for a moment. "No, I know for certain that it wasn't because we later annexed Hawaii and the Philippines. I'm pretty sure that's not what was originally intended by 'Go West, young man,' but that's how it ended up—way, way out West."

"Did it end with the West?" Tatanka asked, his fiery eyes glowing with greater intensity than when the conversation had first begun.

"No, again," Jim mused aloud. "It just turned southward. That's what the Monroe Doctrine was all about, and the Roosevelt Corollary. Kicking all of the European powers out of the Western Hemisphere and sort of policing Central and South America."

"Did it end there?" Tatanka's eyes sparkled but lost none of their fierceness.

Before Jim had a chance to respond, a vision filled his mind's eye. He could see his father's antique, tarnished globe that used to sit on the shelf above his roll-top desk with an ornate compass rose placed squarely in the center of the outline of the United States. Gradually, the arrows pointing north, south, east and west began to grow out from the compass and encircle the globe in every direction, reaching and stretching all the way around until they reconnected on the other side of the world.

Jim stood speechless as the scene began to fade out and eventually vanish into thin air. He had never seen a vision in his life and was mesmerized by the image which now seemed to be permanently etched into his psyche.

"I believe we are done here," Tatanka said resolutely. "You will be visited by more of my friends, so be ready. As for now, go in peace and tread softly."

With that, the great beast was gone, and the rhythm of the airport with all of its noise and its hustle and bustle instantly returned to normal, leaving Jim feeling like he had just emerged from underwater or as if he had suddenly been awakened from an epic dream.

He had no idea how much time had passed or if time had moved at all, but at that moment, he heard the final boarding announcement for his flight and knew he didn't have time to sit around and process all that had just occurred. He swooped up his carry-on, straightened his ball cap, and rushed to the gate entrance where he handed his ticket to the neatly dressed gate attendant and boarded his flight.

III

Once he had settled into his seat on the plane, Jim took a long, hard, deep breath and sunk his head into the leather headrest. He craned his neck back and stared at the ceiling for a long time before he noticed the stewardess standing right next to him in the aisle, leaning toward him slightly.

"Would you like anything to drink?" she asked after finally garnering his attention.

He paused for a moment and fumbled in his mind through his choices before finally blurting out, "Whiskey on the rocks." He instantly felt proud of himself as if he had made some monumental policy decision and added a "thank you" to further tip the scales in his favor. He was truthfully amazed that his mind still had any functionality left after such a bizarre and surreal encounter.

As he sank down into his seat, his mind began to wander,

and without conscious recollection, it drifted off into the memory of a haunting performance of *A Christmas Carol* that he had seen as a child in an old playhouse in Savannah, GA— the noise of the clanking chains of the Ghost of Christmas Past ringing in his ears. The eerie yet rhythmical sound had plagued his dreams for weeks after the show and had speckled his thoughts on occasion since, particularly around the holiday season. But that was fantasy, and this was real. Or at least he thought it was real. It certainly *felt* very real. But how could it be? It had been years since his one and only soiree with hallucinogenic drugs, and even then, that experience paled in comparison to this, like a statue does to a live model or a shadow to the object that cast it.

There was substance to this encounter—as bizarre as it was—a certain weightiness that he could not fully describe or wrap his head around. But in his heart, he knew that something significant and almost eternal had transpired and that he would not be able to discount it easily. And although he dreaded it at the core of his being, he could not help but hope that Tatanka's prediction would come true, that he would have another visitation from one of its colleagues as the great beast had put it.

By now the stewardess had returned with his drink, so he picked up the glass and raised it just high enough to catch the shimmer of the dark amber liquid in the sunlight streaming through the small, oval window. Jim tilted the glass, downing the liquor in two sharp gulps, then closed his eyes and allowed his mind to drift.

As the governor of the great state of Georgia, Jim spent a

whole lot of time in the air, both for work and with his family. He never slowed down much, and even his vacation time stampeded forward at a grueling pace, his family always straining to keep up and wondering if their time together even counted as a break, inevitably returning home more tired than when they left.

Jim had always been hard charging. He grew up hunting, fishing, and doing all things outdoors in the foothills of the Appalachian Mountains. His family home bordered nearly 200 acres of undeveloped land that he had resolved as a boy to explore and utilize every square inch of. He hated sitting still but knew it was part of the conquest of bringing home a trophy buck or the biggest trout of the summer, so he learned how to wait without ever losing sight of the prize.

Jim carried in his very being a diligence unlike any his parents had ever seen. From a young age, Jim's determination to be the best was only surpassed by the pragmatic and detailed plans he drew up to actually achieve whatever audacious goal happened to be in his sights at the moment. When he was only seven years old, he took it upon himself to learn archery, and after practicing day and night all summer long, he could easily outshoot both of his brothers, who were two and four years older than him respectively.

At the age of nine, Jim drew up a schematic for a "Boys Only" tree house and somehow convinced his older brothers to build it for him, using leftover plywood from when his father had replaced the barn roof and paying for the labor with the money he had earned milking the cows every morning at 5 a.m., a job he had held since he was six. His brothers were too lazy to hold the milking job consistently, and one time when his oldest brother tried to edge him out, Jim undercut him until he had his monopoly back and then slowly hiked his wage back up to its original rate.

His mother thought it was a funny and peculiar sight to see a boy that small bossing his older brothers around like the foreman on a worksite, but that was Jim. The reason why he wanted to build the tree house in the first place was so that he could escape the nuisance of his nagging baby sister, who always somehow got a hold of his model airplanes and shook them violently until all of the intricate parts he had meticulously painted and glued together began to fly off in all directions like little pieces of shrapnel raining throughout the house. His father was never around to hear out his strikingly eloquent yet somewhat emotional appeals for justice, and his mom always sided with his sister. "She's only a baby, Jimmy," she would say in her soothing voice which she never raised for any reason aside from when the boys tracked mud into the house. "She'll grow out of it."

Jim thought she grew *into* it more and more each day, and he would huff off in a tizzy upon the denial of his latest appeal to go pick up the scraps and remnants of an F4 fighter jet or whatever model he happened to be working on at the time. He used the tree house once it was built to house his model airplanes as well as his large collection of die cast cars, which he liked to arrange in intricate patterns like traffic frozen in time on the freeway.

Once Jim had finished with it, the tree house looked more like a museum than a boys' clubhouse, but that's the way he liked it. And since he had financed its construction, he always had the final say-so. His brothers ultimately learned to leave Jim alone for the most part, since he was so convincing that his arguments would often turn their own positions against whatever it was they were lobbying for, and they did not much like that, being outwitted by their brat kid brother.

In his college years, Jim became a political force to be reckoned with, once organizing a campus wide sit-in to demand the resignation of the president of his university over an expense-account scandal, a story which he personally investigated and broke in the school newspaper. Due to his role in staging the protest, he was the first student in his university's history to participate as a voting member of a presidential search committee, and he used his newfound notoriety on campus to springboard into his election as student body president the following year.

His launch into politics out of college had both a tragic and fortuitous twist. After serving as a summer intern for a state congressman, the chief of staff suffered a sudden, massive heart attack and Jim, being the only intern who had not returned to college for the fall, was thrust into the slot temporarily. It only took two months for the congressman to decide to keep him on full-time, and Jim became the youngest congressional chief of staff on the hill.

Five years later, Jim won a seat in the Georgia State Senate from District 40, representing the Atlanta metro area. He made a name for himself opposing the merger between Georgia Power and the Savannah Electric and Power Company, which would have created an electric utility monopoly across the state. The deal was backed by the Atkinson family who had owned and operated the Georgia Railway and Power Company all the way up to the Atlanta transit strike in 1950 and who owned a slew of telecom and gas utility companies throughout the Southeast.

Jim coupled his innovative organizing power with his un-faltering tenacity, along with a splash of Southern charisma, to get bipartisan support for a bill to halt the merger at a time when the two sides of the isle weren't even looking at each other, much less collaborating together. Despite intense cor-porate pressure, the merger remained effectively blocked for the next three decades.

After serving two terms in the State Senate, Jim ran for Lieutenant Governor and won by a landslide. His career took another providential turn when, shortly after his election, the Governor was tapped for a cabinet position in DC, and at the age of 37, with a young wife and two small children, Jim Ham-ilton moved into the Governor's Mansion.

Suddenly, Jim was jolted by the passenger next to him put-ting on his jacket, and he realized that he had fallen asleep. He looked out the window and saw that the plane had already landed and was taxiing to the terminal. The passengers all around him were fidgeting in their seats like unruly school-boys at the end of a long day, itching to get outside and play in the inviting sunshine. His long sleep had done him good and had acted like a reset button for his nerves. The odd encounter in the terminal was behind him now and felt like nothing more than a distant memory or a faded dream.

He rubbed his eyes thoroughly and groped under his seat for his briefcase, which he quickly located with his hand and retrieved into his lap. Row by row, the passengers in front of him cleared their seats into the main aisle and filed swiftly out of the plane. He followed suit feeling like a domino in a chain reaction that could be set off at any moment. Finally, he reached the threshold of the plane and crossed over into the long, sterilized tube leading to the terminal that always reminded him of the inside of an MRI machine.

Once he emerged from the narrow tunnel into the wide open space of the airport, Jim felt like he could breathe again. He filled his lungs with the air of adventure and began his search for a coffee stand where he could rejuvenate himself. On the way, he checked his phone and discovered a string of messages both from home and the office, all of which he ignored and scrolled past until he came to the one he was looking for. His lover was waiting for him at baggage claim. He did not want to keep her waiting, not for any altruistic purposes but out of simple obedience to the pounding in his chest, so he quickly grabbed a cup of black coffee and began his trek across the terminal.

IV

'Hola, amor."

Jim heard her voice before he saw her face, and everything

inside of him leapt. The smooth and even tone of her voice captured all that he loved about her and embodied the lost romantic idealism that he had craved for so many years—decades even. Instantly, he felt her long nails running down the side of his leg, and his mind was swept into a frenzy. He spun around on a dime and embraced his foreign lover.

His bags came through with no grief, and once they were loaded into her car, Jim and his mistress began the one hour drive to her villa in downtown Barranco. They left the Jorge Chávez International Airport and drove south through Callao past San Miguel down to the Costa Verde, where the Pacific Ocean opened up before them like a vast, shimmering desert. They exchanged only a handful of words the entire ride as the wind splashed through their hair like ripples of raw emotion and anticipation. There was something romantic about the silence, sensual even, and no words were needed to accentuate the electricity in the air that was palpable, as if the words themselves might destroy the moment and shatter it into a million pieces.

They finally reached Barranco with its yellows and pinks and reds splashed against the walls of the buildings and colorful murals tattooing the sides of bridges and restaurants and storefronts. The second floor villa overlooked la Playa Barranquito and was a little slice of heaven all by itself. Once inside, Jim dropped his bags on the floor and chose a comfortable looking recliner to collapse into.

Weary from a long day of travel, he closed his eyes and allowed all of the tension and striving and disguising to wash away in the sound of the rolling waves rising up from the beach below. He did not intend to fall asleep, but his tired body drew his soul into a state of hibernation so quickly that his mind did not have time to stop it.

Shortly after nodding off, Jim awoke with a start, encompassed by a palpable sense of feeling alone. He could still hear the gentle lapping of the ocean waves crashing against the shore, but somehow there was a tangible void, like he was floating aboard a spaceship or like the air had been totally sucked out of the room. He arched his back in the chair and stretched deep with his arms and legs extended as straight as he could manage, then he slowly began to survey his surroundings from end to end.

After a few moments, just as he was preparing to emerge from his impromptu daybed, he heard a shriek unlike anything he had ever heard in his entire life. The sound nearly toppled him backwards out of the recliner. He whipped his head around to see what could have made such a terrible and awesome racket, and he found himself face to face with the largest bald eagle he had ever laid eyes on. The animal was so stately and so imposing that he could not look away, even though something about the animal's intense gaze created an uncomfortable conviction deep inside of him that he longed to run from.

Jim's mind immediately flashed back to his conversation with Tatanka and the great animal's foreboding words about the colleagues who would be visiting him. There was no question in his mind that this was one of them, the beginning of the fulfillment of this strange prophecy.

"Whhh, what do you want with me?" Jim said instinctively without thinking, feeling a tangible fear creep over his entire being from head to toe. His conversation with Tatanka had felt so real at the time, but he had since entertained the idea that it had been nothing more than a dream. But now, the reality of the whole situation came crashing in once again, and he could not deny that he was locked into some very real, yet other-worldly encounter which he could neither escape nor explain.

"My name is Freedom," the great eagle began, slowly but forcefully. "I have come to have a word with you." Just as with his conversation with Tatanka, the words did not seem to emanate from the eagle's mouth, but rather from its mind directly into his.

Jim pivoted in his chair until he was directly facing the fierce-looking creature, and he paused to proverbially pinch himself or to see if he could wake himself up from what was quickly turning into a nightmare. Yet he found himself as awake and alert as he had ever been, almost hyper-aware of his own being and consciousness in a way that he could not totally comprehend or explain if he were to try. All he knew was that every one of the hairs on the back of his neck stretched straight to the sky, and a current of electricity pulsed through his veins like lightning.

"You know why I've come, don't you, Jim?" the majestic eagle questioned.

Jim stared blankly with no recollection of any logical reason why one might ever find themselves in such a predicament as the one he was currently in.

"When you were a young boy, you prayed a prayer," the eagle continued in its stately voice, "and now that prayer is being answered."

Jim racked his brain. It had been years since he had prayed—other than the liturgical formalities of church services and meals and funerals—so he had to jog his memory to unearth the root of this mysterious statement. But as time seemed to have no bearing in this place, he was able to search the annals of his mind without the constant hurry which accompanied most of his brainstorming sessions in the real world.

He also perceived that he was receiving outside help from Freedom itself, and Tatanka too, although the latter was not visibly present, helping him to navigate the corridors of his past to reach the answer that he believed must exist if the great eagle had mentioned it. He danced through rote nighttime routines, rounds and rounds of "Now I lay me down to sleep" before he stumbled upon a memory of something real, something authentic standing out in the gray matter of religious duties and meaningless repetition to appease mom and dad and even his own conscience—although it was a thin veil most of the time.

His mind flitted upon a hazy picture of a prayer circle in a funeral home, a brain file that had not been accessed in decades. Yet as he focused on it, the memory became less vague and slowly but surely came into focus in his mind's eye. He could see himself as a young boy, maybe eight or nine, clinging tightly to his mother's hand, eyes closed fiercely, and he was praying aloud. He had begun out of sheer pretense or a desire to please and impress his family or perhaps just to avoid standing out when it was his turn to pray, but what came out of his mouth and out of his heart was real and genuine, a true and authentic expression to God or to whatever it was that might heed the small words of a small boy growing up in a small town.

He had loved his grandmother and didn't understand why she had been taken from him. His mom said that the doctors had made a mistake, and he wasn't old enough to even begin to comprehend a thought like that. Doctors didn't make mistakes. They were the ones who made everything better. If we could only get to them in time. All he knew was that something had gone terribly wrong and that he would never see his Meemaw again and that he was sad.

As he watched on through the lens of his internal playback, tears began to roll down the small boy's flushed cheeks and his hand gripped that of his mother until the blood flow in her fingers became so restricted that they began to turn purple and crimson.

"God," he squeaked through chest-heaving sobs, "I want to see my Meemaw again. Please let me see Meemaw again."

Suddenly, Jim's consciousness snapped back to the present moment, and he sat face to face with the eagle once again. All of the fear had left his body and a warm blanket of peace and comfort and feeling at home surrounded his being like an aura of pure light. He noticed something that he had not noticed before and now that he thought about it, he couldn't believe that he has missed this detail at first glance (or perhaps it had not been there before). On the feet of the majestic eagle, it wore what looked like two tethers, although upon further inspection, he discovered that they were rusted iron shackles connected by a small iron chain, also stained brown and orange with rust.

"Why do you have those chains?" Jim blurted out before his mind could filter his words.

"Ah," spoke the eagle straight into his mind. "You are cutting directly to the chase, my friend. And let it be established that I do desire to be your friend, Jim. You have nothing to fear in my presence, nor in Tatanka's, nor in the presence of any of our colleagues. This may be a fearful experience to you, only because it is completely unfamiliar—you have no context for this. Yet it is a safe place nonetheless. You have to trust us, Jim, which means that you must step out into a realm that you do not understand. But remember, just because you don't understand something doesn't mean it's not precisely what you need."

Jim pondered these words for a moment before responding. "Yes," he spoke slowly with more intentionality this time. "I do believe you. Your heart, I can feel that your heart is pure. I trust you." He laughed at himself as he said this and took a deep breath that his lungs were aching for and could have used about five minutes ago. He could feel the remaining tension leave his body as he relaxed into his strange yet intriguing circumstance.

"Good. Now that we are comrades—officially—we can begin. You asked about my chains. What are chains used for, in your world?"

Again, Jim thought for a moment. He did not feel pressed to answer right away, and as with his soul searching excursion just moments prior, the normal weight of time and schedule and to-do did not hold any precedent here. He looked deep into the eyes of the bird wearing chains called Freedom and noted the irony as he began to answer, feeling that everything he needed to know was contained wholly within those fiery eyes.

"Chains, I suppose, are for restricting things," Jim spoke, becoming more sure of his voice with each word. "To keep things from moving, to keep them in place. And to protect property, to keep people from stealing things of value, or of perceived value, that is."

"What else?" Freedom probed. "How are they used in human relationships?"

"Well," Jim began again. "They are used to impose one person's will over another, to dominate another person, to prevent them from doing what they want to be doing and to force them to do something else."

"Very good." The eyes of the majestic animal twinkled and blazed as if consumed by fire. "What right does one human being have to put another human being in chains?"

"Let's see," Jim pondered aloud. "In society, there are agreed upon rules and social norms that, when they are transgressed, an individual may have to be removed from a community in order to protect that community, to protect everyone else. Like when someone commits a crime, depending on the severity, they may be put in prison for a time to buffer them from others and to help them understand that their actions are unacceptable, to give them time to change their mind before they reenter society."

Freedom nodded. "Insightful. Would you say that individuals in a particular society have agreed to live by those norms and rules that you mentioned?"

"Yes, of course," Jim continued. "At least tacitly if not explicitly. By living in a certain place, a country or a state or a municipality, an individual automatically agrees to abide by the laws of that land, just by breathing the air. If he doesn't like the agreed upon norms, he ought to just go somewhere else."

"So, prisoners who wear chains wear them, in a sense, by their own volition, by breaking laws which they are fully aware of, laws that are actually intended to protect them as well as those around them?"

"For the most part," Jim said thoughtfully, "there are unjust laws and political prisoners and those who are wrongly convicted, but for the most part, prisoners are individuals who have wittingly broken laws that are designed to protect society and to preserve the common good, laws that they have agreed upon by living in a certain jurisdiction."

"Then," probed Freedom, "what do you call it when an innocent person is put in chains against their will?"

"I call that slavery," Jim said assertively, gritting his teeth just a little bit.

"Yes, Jim. You have discovered my second name—Slavery—and the irony of my chains." The gaze of the great eagle narrowed, and Jim could feel a shift in the atmosphere down to his bones as if a furnace had been lit somewhere deep inside of him.

"When chains are used to restrict the freedom of lawbreakers, they protect the freedom of all. But when they are used to take away the freedom of innocent men and women, they endanger freedom everywhere and ensure that no one can be fully confident in his or her existence as a free person. Did the slaves who were brought to America agree upon any common laws with their captors by living within a certain jurisdiction?"

"Of course not. They were uprooted from their homes, conquered, and placed under the jurisdiction of a completely foreign people in a completely foreign land. They were enslaved."

"And the law of your land allowed for that?"

"Sadly, yes. The entire British Empire was built with slave labor, like most every other empire before it, and the British colonies in North America were no exception."

"Did the United States of America stand as an exception?"

"It does now," Jim huffed, slightly irritated by the affront. "Where are you going with this?"

"Jim, the emblem of your nation stands as a symbol of freedom to some and a symbol of bondage to others. The very documents which secured your freedom simultaneously secured a life of perpetual servitude for an entire race of people in your midst, stolen from their homes and placed in chains against their will, a fate which only a cataclysmic intervention nearly a century later could correct. Your annual celebration of these documents continues to be a day of bitter remembrance for some and a reminder of the dual nature of your creed—all men never truly meant all men."

"What exactly do you mean by that?" Jim asked sharply, still a little annoyed.

"'We hold these truths to be self-evident, that all men are created equal, that they are endowed by their Creator with certain unalienable Rights, that among these are Life, Liberty and the pursuit of Happiness'—what liberty, what happiness do slaves possess?"

"None, I suppose," Jim replied tersely.

"And how many slaves were being held against their will in this nation at the time those words were penned?"

"I don't know," Jim thought, calculating in his head for a second. "Half a million maybe. Those exact figures aren't known."

"Does it matter?" Freedom's tone grew soft. "One is enough. Were these human souls not men? Men and women and children, bearing the likeness and the image of their creator and sharing that same likeness with their very own captors? Words may sound good on paper, inspiring and poetic even. But unless they are lived out in flesh and blood, they are just that—a nice poem."

Jim sat quietly for a moment, turning this thought over in his mind. Suddenly, a question began to brew in his spirit. Reflecting back on his conversation with Tatanka, he gave air to his query in an attempt to connect the dots. "What does this have to do with Manifest Destiny?"

"Manifest Destiny," the eagle continued, "ensured that no one *outside* of your nation who found themselves in your path of conquest would ever be safe. Slavery ensured that no one *inside* of your nation who found themselves with the wrong blood in their veins would ever be safe. Consider the offspring of a white man with a black woman, down to the third generation. Just because your father or grandfather was free didn't ensure that you would be. Just a fraction of slave blood in your veins made you a slave—in their eyes. Yet no one is a slave, that is, no one is *less than*, in the eyes of the Great Spirit."

"Who is this Great Spirit?" Jim blurted out with a gleam in his eyes of eager longing and childlike curiosity.

"You will know soon enough, dear friend," Freedom replied, "but until then, you have a few more appointments to make. Embrace the journey and rest your spirit. You have a long road ahead still."

With these words, the great eagle raised its massive wings as if to fly away and suddenly vanished into thin air. Jim sat mesmerized with the remnant of the vision still burned onto his retinas. He closed his eyes and the outline of the magnificent creature filled a negative space against the black and crimson of his closed eyelids as if he had just stared at the noonday sun for a moment too long.

The conversation had left him with more questions than answers, and he found himself wishing that the apparition had not disappeared so abruptly. Although a deep curiosity held him fast to this strange process facilitated by these almost mythical creatures, Jim simultaneously harbored a biting disdain for the interruption which he had neither invited nor consented to.

"Why me and why *now*?" he brooded to himself with an air of self-pity which he borrowed somewhere from his childhood. He wanted to stamp his foot but knew it wouldn't do any good and thought better of it. Instead, he tried to do what he had been instructed to do, which was to rest his spirit.

What did that even mean anyhow? He had never used language like that before. The only people he knew who talked about spirits were the hokey ghost tour guides who gouge a fortune out of tourists walking around downtown Savannah late at night with their pirate costumes and oversized lanterns. Either way, he knew one thing. Worrying about what came next wasn't going to speed up the process one bit. So he allowed his head to sink back into the recliner as a strange song that he hadn't heard in years came into his mind. It was a song his childhood nanny used to sing, and he could hear it in his ears just as clearly as if she were in the room with him.

Oh, freedom
Oh, freedom
Oh, freedom over me
And before I'd be a slave
I'd be buried in my grave
And go home to my Lord and be free

V

"Jim, Jim."

Jim opened his eyes and found his lover hovering over him

like a mother hen, shaking his shoulders with a gentle grip but firmly enough to awaken him.

"We," she began with enough sass in her voice to defeather a chicken, "are late. Our reservation is in veinte minutos and you, mister sleepyhead, must still to get dressed. Vámonos, mi amor."

Jim leapt to his feet with a start as the blood surged to his brain, causing him to feel a little woozy in the head and tingly all through his extremities. He felt a sudden sense of panic as one does after waking from a very deep sleep, and he snatched his bag off of the floor more abruptly than the moment necessitated.

He scampered off to his bedroom to freshen up and change, knowing that he would be expected to look his very best and admitting to himself that deep down he wanted the same for the sake of the occasion. Jim had long ago adopted a no-nonsense approach to getting dressed up (as with everything else he did in life), adding one piece of clothing at a time in meticulous fashion, in meticulous order.

Efficiency is what makes the world turn, he told himself as he buttoned his shirt. *Mother Nature doesn't slow down for weakness. She just swallows it up and never looks back.*

Jim was a handsome man and had been since he was a teen, ever since the rest of his body had grown into his gangly limbs, with narrow but strong cheekbones, a sleek and aggressive jaw, and a head full of wavy salt and pepper hair. He had learned as a youth the importance of standing up straight, or rather it had been hammered into the depths of his soul by his overbearing father, who resembled a drill sergeant more than a dad you wanted to go fishing with or confide in.

Jim held himself with an air of respectability and a certain poise that you typically find only in royalty, which his family could nearly vouch for in the American sense having descended from a long line of wealthy plantation owners. He had spent his summers at his family's plantation on the Savannah River and would often recall with fondness swimming in the snake infested waters without a drop of fear running through his veins. In those days, kids played hard until they were bruised and sore, and shoes were not even a topic of conversation, not in the wild summertime.

Jim had nearly finished his dressing process and was adjusting his suspenders, when he heard a light rap at the bedroom door.

"Come on, my love, rápidamente!"

Jim's checks instantly grew flushed as a moment of righteous indignation overtook him at what he would have considered at home to be an unpardonable insult. He was moving forward with maximum efficiency and had been getting ready as fast as humanly possible since he had hustled out of the living room not even 10 minutes ago. Yet he found that here, in this world alone with his lover, he had more patience than he did at home, and he held his tongue. He took a deep breath and allowed the blood to drain out of his cheeks.

"Yes, mi amor," he answered almost sweetly, with only a hint of agitation lingering in his voice.

This would have been an impossible feat in his home, in his

marriage, and he knew it all too well. An explosion of words and temper and self-defense would have been sure to flow through the closed door if his wife had produced a similar slight, usually loud enough for the children to hear, which would inevitably set off a chain reaction from her at upsetting the whole house over nothing. His nerves, he had always found, were the rawest at home, among those he claimed to love the most. His family looked great on a campaign postcard but failed under the litmus test of contentment and even sheer civility at times.

In the back of his mind, Jim wrestled with the thought—or was it undeniable reality?—that he was running away from something, a state of constant self-loathing and misery, rather than to something, a love he found beautiful and inspiring. Yet every time the thought threatened to check his whimsical patterns of self-sabotage, he immediately and forcefully overpowered it with a barrage of premeditated justification and romantic ideals that he had formulated over the years of living in a vacuum of utter longing, a checklist which carried overtones of truth but that was hopelessly out of touch with the reality of politics and life and raising a family.

Jim straightened out his black bowtie one final time and gave himself a look in the mirror that was both fierce and unafraid. He had never let those persistent naggings in the back of his mind stop him before, and he wasn't about to start now. He threw open the pocket door that divided him and his mistress causing a loud bang that shook the villa, and he launched himself out into the evening.

VI

As Jim leaned out over the rail of the Lima Marina Club, he felt as if his body was hovering over the vast expanse of the Pacific which lay before him, beads of sweat still dripping down the sides of his forehead. *Now this is dinner and dancing,* he thought with a sense of smug satisfaction like a Wild West outlaw who had defied the odds and the wanted posters to ride off into the sunset with the loot *and* the girl.

He closed his eyes and tilted his head back slightly, just enough to allow the ocean breeze to pick up his hair and run through it like a pack of wild horses, tossing the undulating strands this way and that. His shirt was soaked through with perspiration and stuck to his tired body providing a wave of coolness with each gust of salty air, the thrill being that he did not know whose sweat it was.

These were the moments that dispelled all of the doubts, like a baseball soaring out of the park in the bottom of the 9th, the unmistakably clear snapshots in time that charted the course forward for men like James David Hamilton the Fifth, who knew what had to be done and who executed the game plan at all costs, always coming through in the heat of the moment.

As he stood soaking up the air of victory and conquest, Jim felt a violent shaking move through his entire body from bottom to top, like the boards underneath his feet were going to split in two. He was instantly thrown to the ground and barely had time to pull his forearms up over his head to prevent his face from hitting the wood of the deck.

Although he had impacted the ground with great force, he

experienced no pain anywhere in his body. As he lay on the deck in almost a fetal position, he felt the air grow completely still all around him as a sense of inexorable peace overwhelmed him. There was no more shaking, no movement at all, just an eerie stillness that reminded him of the early morning fishing trips of his childhood on the lake when the water lay motionless, beyond placid, and he was the only person for miles around.

Jim was hard-headed, and self-admittedly so, but he was beginning to recognize the signs, or rather the feeling, of these otherworldly encounters which suddenly seemed to be following him everywhere he went. The shift was not external in nature but felt like a spike in his internal barometric pressure alerting him that a storm was on its way. Time, or rather his perception of it, ground to a sudden halt, and Jim became keenly aware of his inner voice and the moral debate which raged on constantly inside of his soul, a dialogue he tried to suppress the majority of the time, but which he could not presently ignore.

Why me? Jim sulked to himself as he lay motionless on the ground. *Why now of all times, in the middle of a perfect night— of my perfect night?*

Something inside of him told him to roll over onto his left side, and after a few moments of wondering if he could even move his body at all, he attempted the maneuver, finding that he was able to execute it without any difficulty or discomfort whatsoever. From this new position, he found an easy way to rotate his torso to bring himself into a seated position, and as soon as he was upright, he felt a strong gust of air against his face, causing him close his eyes for just a moment. Once he reopened them, he found himself sitting in front of a sleek bird about a foot and a half tall that resembled a raven with jet black feathers.

Jim instinctively drew himself back, pulling his legs into his chest and inadvertently finding a rather comfortable way to sit as he prepared for yet another strange dialogue. Jim thought that the timelessness of these encounters would be the hardest thing to describe, if he ever ended up confiding in anyone. It was tangible, like a material substance encompassing his entire body, insulating him from the racing thoughts and external stressors of the mean work-a-day world he knew all too well.

He could not tell if time had stopped altogether or if it had sped up so fast that it suddenly became imperceptible, but in either case, it made him feel almost weightless, like all of the burdens and the bills and the baggage of life were lifted in a single instant. It's not that they were gone altogether—just distant enough that he wasn't able to focus his attention on them. Even if he were to try with all of his might, he felt it would be impossible to take his mind off of the present, the singular moment at hand.

"Jim," croaked the bird in a much deeper and more imposing voice than he would have expected from such a small bird. "You know why I've come."

"Well, as a matter of fact," Jim replied sharply, "I don't have a, I don't have a godda—"

Jim tried to complete the word that was hanging on the tip of his tongue, but it would not materialize. His mouth was totally frozen in place until his mind landed on a different word, an alternative neurological pathway to communicate his thought. He instantly became aware of a deep, burning anger that had overwhelmed him in the moment, and he made an attempt to placate himself before moving forward. He knew that time alone would not work in this place to overcome his rage, not in the way he used it at home to regain his composure without actually addressing the root of the issue, the exposed nerve itself. Here, he realized that he would have to go deeper.

He took a long draw of the weighty air and quieted his mind, tapping into the inner dialogue which he was still intensely aware of, listening inwardly for just a moment. Instantly, he knew in the core of his being that a new level of humility was needed before he could continue. He did not know how he knew—he just knew.

He sighed deeply and wrestled with his thoughts for an idea of how to do such an abstract thing, to humble oneself, although he was simultaneously aware that he did not possess even a shred of selfless motive in the process, only a desire to get past this mental roadblock which had momentarily paralyzed his thinking. Jim waited and waited, but nothing changed, and he finally came to the conclusion that he had to act, that he must do something, say something, even if he wasn't completely sure what that something was.

"I'm sorry," he finally blurted out to the bird, who was waiting patiently for his response. "It's just that, you see, it's just that I *don't* know why you've come and I *don't* know why I'm here with you and why you, or it, the Great Spirit or whatever, has chosen me for this freaky science experiment, or whatever you want to call it, and—and I could use some answers. Am I making myself clear?"

"Very clear," responded the black bird in the same powerful yet patient voice as before. "Your anger is clouding your thinking, Jim, and you must let it go. These conversations may be an inconvenience for you, or that is your perception, but it is imperative that we continue with this, how did you put it, freaky science experiment."

Jim could not exactly tell, but it appeared that the bird delivered this last line with a bit of a chuckle, although the shift in its intonation was almost imperceptible.

"Alright," Jim breathed out with an impatient sigh, "I said I was sorry. I do trust your process and I guess I believe—well, I believe you have something for me, something that I need. Let's just get on with it, can we?"

"Let's," responded the bird with poise as it shimmied its feathers slightly and lifted its breast and head together to give it an even statelier appearance than before, which produced an odd effect, to witness a bird looking somehow dignified.

"My name," crooned the sleek black bird with a twinkle in its eyes, "is also Jim. Jim Crow. Or as some call me, Jumpin' Jim Crow. Are you familiar with the term?"

The crow bowed its head ever so slightly as it asked the question, communicating a truly inquisitive intent with no hint of condemnation or bitterness, which from Jim's experience often accompanied the subject at hand. In fact, this was the very reason he avoided talking and even thinking about Jim

Crow at all costs, because of the bitter root of guilt and shame which seemed to be its perpetual bedfellow.

"I know that Jim Crow is dead and gone," Jim picked up swiftly. "We've corrected it, moved on, from it and from slavery. And maybe," he hung on this note for just an extra moment creating a dramatic pause, "it's time you did, too."

Jim felt a sense of smug satisfaction come over him as he delivered this last line, as if he had finally gotten a shot in on one of these odd creatures, all of whom seemed to project an aura of complete impenetrability.

"I cannot very well get over what *I am*, Jim," the crow responded with a playful cadence in its voice. "What makes you think that we have moved on and corrected, as you put it, the horrible evils of slavery and Jim Crow?" Although the crow's intonation turned serious, there was again no hint of resentment or spiteful edge that Jim could pick up on, only a soft straightforwardness which elicited an honest response, communicating a sort of tacit permission for Jim to speak his mind without the normal social filters which governed his tongue at all times both as a politician and as a Southerner.

"Well, for starters," Jim began intentionally as if to air a grievance which he had never been provided the opportunity to formally file, "Jim Crow ended more than 50 years ago, and slavery was abolished more than 150 years ago. I see everyone dredging up what is now ancient history and nobody wants to look at what's going on today. I've never owned a slave. I've never lynched anybody or tried to intimidate anybody or used the 'N' word to anybody's face. I just go about my business and try to treat everybody the same. *Everybody*. I've got friends who are black and who are white. I've got voters who are black and who are white. I say it's time to let dead dogs lie."

The little black bird paused for a moment as still as death, and Jim wondered if it was even breathing at all. Then it lifted its head and spoke.

"Thank you, Jim. Your honesty is refreshing. When our feelings on any particular subject are suppressed, they begin to fester and ooze like an open sore. But when we air our grievances and share our hearts openly, those wounds are given the oxygen they need to heal. I do not agree with everything that you've shared, but I do honor your perspective and appreciate your curtness. Let me ask you this, has anyone in your family every owned a slave?"

"Yes, of course, down the line somewhere. But I don't know who, and I really don't care."

"Even if they hadn't, tell me this. What were African slaves brought to the British colonies in North America for, that is, what was their purpose?"

"To work the land—and to take the heat, at least in the South."

"Yes, but why were they forced to work the land? What was the end game?"

"To grow crops. To make money."

"Money, ah yes, but there is something more. Were the investors who underwrote colonial America trying to earn money to make ends meet, to buy groceries for the week, or did they have a greater motive?"

"Well, they were trying to build equity, to extract as much wealth from the colonies, from their investment, as possible. Who do you think paid for all of those ships and expeditions? Somebody's got to make some dough on the whole thing."

"Wealth, precisely. And the colonists, who deeded them the land to live and to work on?"

"The investors and their corporations. And the British government, well, all of it was sort of backed by the Motherland."

"And how did these investors and their corporations and the British government acquire the land which they then deeded out?"

"Well," Jim couldn't help but chuckle at the response which immediately came to mind, "they just showed up."

"And they fought," the crow added without slackening his pace. "They didn't just show up. They showed up armed. Now tell me, who sold the African slaves to the merchants who ultimately brought them to America?"

"Their own da—" Jim stammered as his word choice once again hindered his articulation. "Their own people, which leads me to another good reason why this whole thing is—"

"Jim," the crow interrupted. "Your anger. Your anger is getting you in trouble again. You must learn to be still and you must forgive."

"Forgive?" Jim raised his eyebrows and unwittingly made a sour face. "Forgive who? These people are all dead and gone, you can't forgive someone who is dust."

"Yes, you can, friend. Just think about your father. What's the first thing that comes to mind?"

"That son of a bi—" Jim began and again halted abruptly.

"See, your father has been dead for 15 years. Yet your heart is full of rage and hatred toward him. You *can* forgive the dead, and you must. Forgiveness does not depend on the recipient—it only depends on you. It is a gift from the Great Spirit to release those who have hurt us in the past so that they don't continue to hurt us in the present and into the future. It is a complete release of our offenses so that we can live our days in peace."

"So you're saying my father is totally off the hook for the utter misery he put me, and all of us, through?"

"No, Jim. I am not saying that at all. Everyone meets justice one way or another. What I am saying is that you are not responsible for executing that justice. When you forgive, you release that person to the justice of the Great Spirit. And you have to trust that he will do a better job of it than you ever could. You have been carrying your hatred for your father around with you for 15 years. He still has a firm grip on you. It's time to release him so that your next 15 years can be a different story, or rather a new chapter."

Jim did not like this response and sulked inadvertently for several moments as he thought of his rebuttal. But as no words came to mind, he just sat and scoured at the bird who seemed to be smirking at him, making light of his misery.

"Jim," the bird picked up with a much softer tone than before, "I am not here to hurt you in any way, but only to help you and to set you free. Forgiveness is a choice that only you can make. The Great Spirit will never force you or anyone to forgive or to do anything else for that matter. It is his offer to you—his gift to humanity."

Jim paused for a long while as he replayed scene after scene from his childhood, and from his adulthood, of his father's alcoholic rampages and the wreckage he always left in his path, everywhere he went with seemingly everyone he encountered. Jim swore he would never grow up to be like him. And he swore that he would never forgive him. He was too chicken to take matters into his own hands, although he would replay the memories again and again in his mind, imagining himself standing up to his old man and taking the frying pan right out of his weathered hand and beating him against his side and all over his body, standing between him and his mother who usually received the worst of the blows.

He had no idea how long he fumed and fantasized, whether it was five minutes or five hours, but suddenly a thought came to him that caused his anger to turn inward. He could not believe he had allowed himself to relive this horror for 15 long years.

"I forgive him," he blurted out without even really knowing what he was saying. It was like the unspeakable tension in the earth that suddenly opens up into a fissure, instantly relieving the pressure but leaving the ground cracked in two. Tears welled up in his eyes as Jim began to weep uncontrollably. Violent sobs shook his whole body as he felt the mounting pressure of a lifetime slip away into nothingness. He could not believe he had held on this long on the one hand, and on the other, he could not believe that he had finally forgiven his father.

Jim wiped his tears away with his sleeve as the floodwaters quickly began to abate, although his body still shook as little waves of dry sobs rolled across his torso like aftershocks.

A certain stillness hung in the room as all the cares of the world seemed to lift, and Jim felt peace in his heart for the first time in as long as he could remember.

"Now," the crow eased in, breaking the long pause in their dialogue, "Shall we continue?"

"I'm not sure," replied Jim, regaining his composure and wiping his eyes one last time. "Where exactly are we going with all of this?"

"We are getting to the root," the crow replied. "Slavery in the British colonies and in the fledgling nation of America was a juggernaut of wealth creation based on a system of violence and brutal force. The land was taken violently, and the labor was extracted violently. This was the accepted system of the day, the societal norms which ruled in people's hearts. When slavery ended, Jim Crow became the norm. It was nothing new, nothing earth shattering. Just the same system of violence to ensure that labor remained cheap and that the economy remained strong."

"But how can you say that Jim Crow was the same system as slavery? There were no chains and no whips. Those were free men, free to do whatever they wanted to do, free to go back to Africa if they wanted to."

"Free in a legal sense, sort of, but not in an economic one. Yes, former slaves had the freedom to leave the plantation, but with only enough food and supplies to last them a couple of days, how far could they be expected to go? They certainly didn't have any kind of fare to go back to Africa, much less one state over. Plus, most of them couldn't read, write or do basic math, so they had no power to negotiate or even interpret their ledger as a sharecropper or as domestic help or doing whatever job they were able to find. And with vagrancy laws in place, former slaves who couldn't find work were locked up and farmed out on chain gangs to do the hardest and most menial, backbreaking labor—once again shackled against their will. So one way or the other, they mostly all ended up working for nothing, just like before.

"What you must understand about freedom," the crow continued, "in the way your constitution defines it—life, liberty and the pursuit of happiness, or life, liberty and *property* as John Locke put it—is that freedom is not free. Why were the colonizers free to build wealth on American soil, to pursue their own happiness and property ownership, the very prospect which attracted most early settlers in the first place?"

"Well," Jim spoke up as a thought came to his mind, "in a sense because they had better firepower than the previous tenants. Guns trumped tomahawks and bows and arrows. And because they established communities which protected and allowed individuals to build equity—walled cities at first and laws to protect their assets—a system which was enforced by that very same firepower."

"Precisely. Guns, walls and laws. The more wealth you own, the more recourse you need to protect that wealth. The man with a little money under his mattress may only need four walls, a six shooter and a couple of good ordinances ensuring his property rights, that is, his right to shoot anybody who breaks in to steal his cash. But when you have vaults and vaults full of gold bars, you need Fort Knox to protect it. Yet what do you do when your property is another human being? What do you think enabled the colonists to capture and keep an army of chattel slaves?"

"It's pretty much the same idea," Jim reflected. "Guns and chains. And strong laws to enforce ownership."

"Yes, but there is one additional element needed. Gold can't steal your gun and shoot you with it. How do you protect your property and protect yourself *from* your property when your property is another person?"

Jim sat in silence for a few moments, unsure what the crow was angling at.

"What kept the slaves on the plantations prior to the Civil War and the blacks in their place during Jim Crow was not chains or even the guns themselves. It was the constant, invisible threat of unspeakable violence which loomed over every wrong step, every wrong word and even every wrong look. Jim, the freedom to create wealth on foreign soil with forced labor is not a God-given right. It is a right of the strong. And the brutal. In order to harness the power of a human being, you must first break his will. Brutal retaliation against all insurrection—the whip and the lynching tree—is what made slavery work, and it's what oiled the gears of Jim Crow.

"And if you are willing to open your ears and your eyes, my friend," the crow cocked its head and stared hard into Jim's spellbound eyes, "you will see that it is what continues to grease the wheels of your beloved nation to this day."

With that, the crow vanished into thin air right before Jim's eyes. Jim kept his gaze fixed on the spot where the bird had just been and refused to blink, afraid he might miss something. After half a minute passed and nothing happened, Jim relaxed his stare but only slightly. He looked around slowly for any signs of movement like someone does after they have killed a mosquito to see if any of its cohorts are still around, and seeing nothing out of the ordinary, he began his slow and rather creaky ascent from the deck floor where he had been sitting.

Once again, he had no concept of how long he had been sitting there and felt that it could have been hours or days or perhaps only a few seconds. He wondered what the status of his date would be when he returned and hoped that he had not been gone from reality for too long. As he began his brisk walk from the edge of the dock back to the restaurant with his legs still tingling as the blood returned to normal circulation, he heard him name being called in quite dramatic—Peruvian fashion.

"Jim! Oh, Jim!" his mistress exclaimed with a mixture of excitement and dread in her voice. "Oh, Jim, where on this earth have you been? I have been looking all over for you, mi amor, but I should to have known you would come here, with how you much love the water. Oh, Jim, come and hold me, please!"

Jim wrapped his arms around his distraught mistress and began to console her with placating whispers in her ear and soft fingers running through her hair. Gradually, her heart rate returned to normal, and he could feel her body melt into his as the stiffness completely fled from her posture.

"How long was I gone?" Jim spoke, breaking the silence after a long pause.

"You said you were going to use the baño and then you never return. It has been, well, diez minutos, at least."

Ten minutes, Jim marveled to himself. *Ten minutes.* What had seemed like an eternity of time and emotion and struggle had been packed into a completely insignificant amount of perceptible time. He drew a deep breath of the salty ocean air as he looked to the sky for a brief moment, and then he gently took hold of her hand and led her back to the restaurant.

VII

The next day exploded from the moment Jim woke up into a flurry of activity, making all of the preparations needed for a full day of sightseeing for him and shopping for her. His trips to see his mistress were never cheap, but truthfully he did not mind. Money had never been much of an issue for him, but what hung constantly like an albatross around his neck was the lack of substance in his relationships, both at home and at work.

He could never quite put his finger on the root of the emptiness he often felt in his gut, whenever he slowed down enough to feel anything at all. His interactions seemed to be so bogged down in the mire of formality and surface level exchange that, like a box of saltine crackers, they filled his belly for a moment but left him hungry only minutes later.

There was no shortage of words and conversation and personal contact in Jim's life. In fact, it was quite the opposite. His days were often a barrage of larger-than-life personalities and interesting characters that one could write whole tomes about. Yet the nagging loneliness which followed him through the peaks and valleys of his long, arduous days and seasons of life never seemed to abate. The constancy of it plagued him like his very own shadow, which he knew he would never be able to shake or get free from even for a moment.

The ever-present awareness that he was ultimately alone in a sea of people who were the envy of the world yet as flimsy as origami dolls went to bed with him at night and awoke with him in the morning like a plague worse than death. Yet life ticked on and there seemed to be no escape from the suffocating reality save one, which he could never share with anyone but his foreign lover. The secrecy and depth of planning and cover-up might seem extravagant to an onlooker, but Jim knew that no one would ever fully appreciate the absolute necessity of this lifeline for him. Without it, he was sure that he would suffocate, any minute really. This was his one outlet, his only way to breathe in the fresh and wild air of life.

While his lover shopped, Jim sat at a table outside of Luccio Caffe in Larcomar, a mall built into a cliff wall overlooking the Pacific Ocean in the Miraflores district of Lima, sipping a strong black cup of Peruvian coffee. Patience was possible here and so was peace, virtues that proved utterly unattainable at home. As he watched the waves rhythmically crashing over the sandy beach below, he could feel his heartbeat slow and his emotions level out like a rollercoaster coming to a halt at the end of a long day of frenetic activity.

A nagging feeling of guilt had plagued him earlier in the morning as he had walked along the Malecón to start his day, each step revealing a new and colorful angle of the morning sun reflecting off of the Pacific, that his family was not here with him, that he could never share this moment with his wife and children—ever. Deep down, he felt a strong and devoted love for them and longed to show them the beauty and mystery of life, but his hectic schedule and his inability to connect at a meaningful level when they did finally get to spend time together always hovered over them like a glass ceiling which he could never seem to successfully penetrate.

Perhaps, it was the sheer blinding pace of his "work hard, play hard" lifestyle that he had adopted as a sort of personal mantra in his college years. *Life is too short to live it half-heartedly,* he would repeat to himself almost like a bedtime prayer when his tired head would hit the pillow at night. It had worked so well when the children were young—ski trips out West, jaunts to the BVI, sightseeing in Europe, all connecting the dots between the long weeks and months which stole him away for work—but somewhere along the way he had lost them, and his wife, too.

Her glances at him were so cold, like the biting inescapable frost of a Northeast winter, cutting him to pieces with a single look, leaving his soul completely irreparable and his heart like a puddle on the floor. He had created this. He had done it to himself. He knew it deep down. But it was too far gone now, and at this point, the only path forward was to find moments of escape and retreat—moments just like this one.

After leaving Larcomar, Jim dropped his mistress off at an art gallery uptown and parked near La Marina Lighthouse in Miraflores. He sauntered through the park surrounding the towering edifice, drinking in the smell of the flowering Heliconias and Japanese Honeysuckles, basking in the sounds of children running through the grass, in and out of the tall swaying palm trees, climbing on park benches and statues and everything else not meant for climbing.

Jim had always been fascinated by lighthouses, their prominent height and steady functionality. It saddened him deeply that the simple rhythmic patterns of light had no more use in our modern world than wooden toys and paper roadmaps and all of the now obsolete things he had grown up on as a boy. He often wondered at what point *he* would become obsolete, or if perhaps he already had, and when he would be discarded with all of the other worn out folks into a nursing home somewhere and promptly forgotten.

As Jim approached the soaring black and white striped monument to a forgotten era of nautical dominance and mechanical glory, he noticed something he had never seen before. The black wooden door at the base of the lighthouse stood slightly ajar. He had never heard of anyone offering tours of the tower and had always seen the door closed and locked. He looked around to see if anyone else seemed to notice, but the children continued running and playing with complete abandon and no one appeared to be paying any mind to the door.

Jim slowly approached the door and gave the handle a tug only to find that it opened with the greatest of ease. He quickly slipped inside the threshold and pulled the heavy door behind him to precisely the same position as he had found it. He squinted through the thick darkness as his eyes adjusted to the damp and dimly lit vertical corridor. After a few moments, he could make out the silhouette of a spiral staircase which twisted and wound all the way to the top of the 70 foot iron structure. He was not sure if he had enough guts to make the climb without any invitation or permission other than a barely cracked door, but just as he was contemplating his next course of action, he heard a voice echoing down the chamber from above.

"Come up here," the voice descended like the gentle whisper of a summer breeze.

Jim froze stiff. He had seen and heard so much in the past two days that he wasn't sure what was real anymore. He listened keenly, not making a movement or even taking a breath. He waited for the voice to see if it would speak again, and just as he was about to give up and start breathing, he heard the same faint echo.

"Come up here, Jim."

Jim was spooked. *How in the world could this lighthouse keeper possibly know my name? Does he know, about me, about the affair?* At this thought, Jim wanted to turn and run, but something held him fixed. Before he knew it, his legs were carrying him up, ascending the spiral staircase one step and one rotation at a time, each lap getting closer and closer to the lookout at the top of the light.

Before he knew it, he stood face to face with another door, also painted black but slightly shorter and more narrow than the first. He drew up his hand to knock, but before he could, the door swung open just enough to allow a narrow slit of light out from the heart of the lighthouse. The light exploded the darkness and suddenly Jim could see the iron hull much more distinctly, realizing that it was not black as he had suspected but rather a dark navy blue.

He hesitated for just a moment to survey his surroundings with the help of this extra peek of light and then slowly eased open the mysterious door before him. Light suddenly flooded his world, and he instinctively drew his forearm over his eyes to protect his shocked pupils as they rapidly adjusted to the correct aperture setting. Blinding light was all he could see for several moments, and then slowly the lantern room came into focus one piece at a time. The first thing that caught his attention was the view through the thick storm panes. Sunlight sparkled off dancing blue as the ocean glittered and glistened in all directions as far as the eye could see.

Inside, he could barely make out the outline of the lamp and lens, which methodically emitted three flashes every 15 seconds, a signal which could be seen at night for probably 20 miles. As his eyes grew more and more accustomed to the brightness of the room, he could begin to see the details of the Fresnel lens with its circular grooves emanating out from small, round focal points, one on each of its six sides. Between the breathtaking view and the childish curiosity of being in a working lighthouse lantern room, Jim had totally forgotten about the voice that had called him by name just a few minutes prior.

After three or four rotations of the lamp inside the lens (which is how one measures time at the top of a lighthouse), Jim noticed a stirring out of the corner of his eye. He broke his gaze away from the gleaming Pacific and turned his eyes to the southeast corner of the room where a large water buffalo emerged from behind the lens, snorting and gently shaking its powerful head as it stamped the ground mildly with its front right hoof. Jim instantly recognized the great beast as a carabao, the national animal of the Philippines, by its stocky build and sickle-shaped horns curving backwards toward the neck. He had spent a summer traveling through the Philippines and Indonesia after graduating from college and had witnessed a carabao race, a spectacle he could never forget if he tried.

"You made it, Jim," the wide, heavy animal brayed at him. Although Jim cognitively knew what was going on, the sheer size and close proximity of the thousand pound animal made his heart skip a beat and keep on skipping until the carabao spoke. Instantly, the moment the words emerged from the animal's mouth (or rather from its mind just as it had been with Tatanka and the rest of the otherworldly creatures), a feeling of all-encompassing peace and absolute tranquility descended down over him like the first sheet of rain that sweeps right through you on the front end of a torrential downpour.

For several minutes, or maybe it was half an hour, Jim sat motionless in total silence and basked in the river of peace that flooded his entire being. Then he remembered the question which had been burning in his heart ever since the prior evening when the crow had departed so abruptly. He wanted to ask it before the flow of the conversation got going and he lost his train of thought, so he quickly blurted it out.

"How is it," Jim pondered aloud, "that you seem to know my thoughts? It's like you know them before I say them, even before I think them, or how do I put it, like you're—like you're actually helping me think them."

The large beast connected with Jim's darting eyes and held them fast, its glowing hazel globes burning into the very depths of his soul with a fierce intensity, yet simultaneously exuding such gentleness that he had a difficult time reconciling it with the enormity of the creature before him. He felt safe in its presence on the one hand, but knew that he was vulnerable on the other hand because the hidden secrets of his heart were laid bare.

"Jim," the carabao began slowly with a breath that most closely resembled a human sigh, "you must understand that the Great Spirit knows all things. He knows all that has been, all that is and all that will be. He knows your thoughts before you think them, your words before you speak them and your steps before you take them. I am an extension of the Great Spirit, a messenger sent by Him, so when you are with me, you are with Him. All wisdom comes from Him, so the thoughts you are referring to—when your mind is opened to understand the mysteries of life—this is the work of the Great Spirit and," he paused for a moment and looked up to the sky, "one of His greatest gifts to mankind, a gift which stems from His infinite love."

"Wait a second," Jim fired back reflexively. "If this Great Spirit of yours knows everything before it happens, what does that make me—a puppet?"

"No, Jim. Just because someone knows something does not mean they cause it to happen. The Great Spirit is outside of time. He knows the choices you will make before you make them, but you are the one who must choose—"

"Choose what?" Jim cut him off hotly. "I haven't chosen anything, and here you are, bothering me on my vacation. You won't leave me alone, you follow me everywhere I go, and I wish," Jim stopped and stared directly into the shimmering eyes of the beast, "I wish you would just get out of my life!"

As soon as the words left his mouth, the carabao vanished into thin air like Jim had awoken from a dream. He looked back and forth around the large lens in the middle of the room and slowly moved all the way around it to make sure that the apparition was truly gone.

"Good riddance," Jim muttered to himself as he released a long, breathy sigh. He looked out of the thick glass panes one final time to soak up the view of the rolling ocean before he descended the spiral staircase back down to the ground floor. He found the door cracked an inch or two just as he had left it and swung it open only enough to slip his body through as he darted out into the blaring sun. He slammed the door behind him partly out of anger and party because he didn't want anyone to report anything suspicious like the door to the lighthouse being left ajar. The last thing he needed on this trip was more trouble.

VIII

Jim spent the rest of the day carting his mistress around from store to store, spending way too much money on a painting and a rug and a lamp for her flat that she said all matched, although he failed to see the connection. He held his tongue of course and knew better than to stir up strife when things were going his way. He had brought a considerable amount of cash with him, which he used for all of the purchases, thinking how nice it was to be off the financial grid as well as the communication one.

He sometimes hated the modern era with a deep hatred that welled up from the core of his being, how his credit card tracked every single purchase and compiled them into one place like a standing indictment against him which could detail exactly how much and how often he splurged on golf clubs or fishing equipment with the single click of a button. *The old timers didn't know how good they had it,* he would brood to himself every time he slid his card for an overpriced cup of coffee. *A pot of coffee over the fire on the open prairie would have done me just fine.*

Of course, Jim had never roughed it in his life, and he knew it. But still, he craved a simpler rhythm of life and imagined that he would be well suited for any hardship that might have come along with it, although the greatest obstacle he knew for certain was boredom which always drove him like a harsh taskmaster back into the frantic swing of things whenever he tried to break free and slow down.

"Let's put these old things aside and—" Jim's voice trailed off as he ran his hand up his mistress' leg, which she quickly batted away, wrinkling her nose at him.

"I want to see just how they look, you pícaro," she remarked with a scoff and a long look down her nose at him. She rotated the lamp in its place on an end table by her brown leather sofa next to the recliner where Jim had slept so soundly after his long day of traveling, and she stared intently at the placement of the rug and then back to the lamp and then to the bare spot on the wall where she had envisioned the painting.

Once again, Jim made an advance, this time wrapping his hands around her waist from behind and whispering in her ear something about the first time they had met, which she tuned out completely as she shimmied out of his grasp, her amateur interior design focus completely undaunted.

"Oh, come on," Jim pleaded in a playful tone. "We've been shopping all day. Why don't we leave everything here until tomorrow and call it a day?"

"Not yet, mister," she began without taking her eyes for a moment off the lamp, which she continued to rotate this way and that with her hand. "I need you to hang this picture, over right there, and you can help me also to vacuum under this rug—the floor is inmundo!"

Frustrated, Jim allowed his tongue get ahead of his filter and let slip, "You're worse than my wife," which he had intended to say to himself but due to her close proximity, the words met her ears like a gunshot blast.

"I'm worse than who?!" she exclaimed as she spun around on a dime and lifted her index finger within inches of his face. Jim stood like a statue frozen in the crosshairs of a violent and unstoppable force of nature that he knew had the power to swallow him up whole as he began to process internally how much his gaffe was going to cost him.

"You come all the way to me here to talk about your wife?" The words pounded into Jim's chest as he could feel the tone of her voice escalating rapidly. "I invite you to stay into my home, and you, you—you say I am like your wife, that perra! You speak always so ugly about her and, and—what do you say about me, Jim, when you are away?"

Jim had no words as he felt all of the blood in his body rush to his face, and he began to feel lightheaded thinking about all of the money he had spent to get there and all of the money he had spent earlier in the day, and inside of himself, deep inside of himself, he cursed his tongue which was the only thing powerful enough to bring it all crashing down in a single moment of time.

"You know, you know how much I—"

"I don't know anything anymore, you scoundrel," she cut him off with tears welling up in her eyes. He moved to comfort her, but she jerked away and pointed sternly to the door.

"Out, out with you!" she managed to eke out, fighting back

the tears. He did not move his feet or open his lips but petitioned with his hands and shoulders for her to reconsider the verdict which she had pronounced with such finality.

"No, Jim," she continued, "not this time. You have fooled me for the very final time." With that, she hid her swollen eyes in her hands and ran off to her bedroom where she violently slammed the door, sending a jolt through the apartment which made the lamp that started all this mess wobble slightly on its base.

Jim stared at the lamp, hating it with all of his might. He hated the lamp and the rug and the painting, but most of all the lamp. It took all of the restraint in his entire body not to knock it to the floor, smashing it into a million pieces. He paused for a moment, and not wanting to be outdone, he snatched up his briefcase from beside the recliner and rushed out the front door, swinging it closed with all of his strength as if he were competing to see who could make the grandest, angriest exit.

Jim stormed down the single flight of steps which led from the villa to the street, and he walked briskly to the Malecón, the cliff-top walkway that he loved which stretched for miles along the Pacific-facing side of Miraflores. All of the peace and the placidity in Jim's spirit was gone, replaced suddenly by the all too familiar anger and rage which seemed to constantly plague his life back at home.

Unbelievable! Jim huffed almost audibly as he paced fervently away from his lover's home with no destination yet in his scope. *That woman, amazing! After all I've done for her.*

Jim kept his head down watching the path as it unfolded before him, and as he walked, he breathed—short, hot breaths like a dog panting in the summer heat to stay cool. They were angry breaths, bitter breaths, like the breaths he breathed after the little scuffles with his wife that had defined their marriage for the past decade or more.

Jim walked aimlessly forward but his thoughts remained behind, replaying scene after scene in his mind, scenes from earlier in the day mingled with memories from his childhood and every era of life in between. Each scenario held a common thread and inevitably at some point in the replay, his whole body would tense up as he reached the part where he could see and hear and feel what he should have said and what he should have done, yet instead his mind mocked and sneered at what he did do and what he did say, leaving him with a pit in his stomach which grew and grew and ached and ached until he had to sit down.

He remembered as a young man, really he was still a boy, when his high school sweetheart walked in on him at a party kissing another girl on a dare, and while everything in him wanted to cry out and explain the situation and gush his bleeding heart to her, the girl of his dreams, he turned and kissed the stranger deeper and harder. He did not know what possessed him to do such a thing, to act in the complete opposite direction his heart told him to go in, except that he had been caught and if he was going to get caught, he might as well go down in flames.

He had always wondered as he had replayed the memory a

million and one times what his life would have been like if she had come into the room one minute earlier or one minute later or if he had had the wherewithal to stop and to reason with her and to beg and plead with her for clemency—would she have relented? Would she have given him another chance instead of smashing his locker in and throwing all of his books and notebooks and papers on the hallway floor at school the next day?

There was no looking back at that point, and his life course was set by his stubborn refusal to forgive her for embarrassing him in that way. He knew it was a cry, a cry for something, for an apology which never came or at least for an acknowledgement of love lost or the beauty of a high school romance sacrificed on the altar of going along with the crowd and too much alcohol and sheer childishness. But she sure wasn't going to get any concessions from him after a public spectacle like that, and Jim immediately set his heart against the love he once had—all for the sake of what? His pride, perhaps, or just the way he had been raised to always get the upper hand and keep it at all costs.

Maybe this is what had led to the complete deterioration of his marriage and, as a result, his family and home life—his stubborn refusal to let anyone or anything get the best of him. His mind flipped to his 10 year anniversary and the two glasses of champagne left in the hotel room by the concierge, the image burned into his memory with two chocolate covered strawberries between them, a decadent gift meant to mark the occasion and highlight love like bits of lace around the collar of an elegant evening gown, like fireworks at the end of a Friday night baseball game, like the rose garden at the far end of the backyard, designed to frame and celebrate something of true value and create a brief touch of the eternal around the transcendent moments of life.

As he carried the tray to the bed, his wife turned and (he could remember it as if it was all happening this very moment) he felt a slight brush against his back, the tray began to tilt as the glasses slid, he reached out his hand but it was too late and their transcendent moment crashed in an explosion of glass and fizz and red and brown stains on the white down comforter, an eruption of motion and frenzy and utter waste.

Jim turned hotly to her and berated his wife for causing such a mess, and in his mind's eye 20 years later, he could see the countenance on her face as vividly as when it was happening change to sadness, and for a long moment the sadness hung on her cheeks and eyes like a sole dark rain cloud on the horizon on the sunniest of days—and what he saw next, her sadness fled as her mouth drew up and a wave of hot anger came over her face as she fired back like a cat in the corner fighting for life and existence and to save face someway and somehow.

It was not in her nature to retaliate, and he knew that he had pushed her over the edge in some way. The years of nips and shots and word arrows flying at her had penetrated the gentleness and the temperance of a truly patient and wholesome woman. Again, just like that moment from his high school days, he wanted to embrace her and scream, "No!" and pour his heart out to her, reassuring her of how much he loved her and how much he hated himself for changing her in this way like water rushing over rocks in a stream, inevitably wearing away at them until they become unrecognizable from their former contour.

He wanted to tell her that it was all his fault and that he wanted to change and that he didn't want to live this way and that it wasn't *her*. But instead his heart turned in the opposite direction and hardened against her, and he flew irreversibly with the hot wind of anger behind him and he dug in his heels. No apology came, just a hard stare and a one liner. "It's your mess, *you* clean it up." And as he left the room, he knew deep down that it would never be the same between them

As he continued to walk, almost frantically now, his mind reverted back to earlier in the day when his mistress was pining over antiques and art like she actually knew something. He knew in reality her pride was rooted in his wallet, the thing that gave her access to this exclusive and elite world, rather than her formidable knowledge. Talk was cheap but $8,000 in cash from his private savings account pulled before he left for the trip gave her a platform everywhere she went with him—yet strangely he resented her for it. As she discussed design and art and history with the various shopkeepers and curators, he found himself wanting to cut her down to size, to assert himself as the benefactor and explain to her how she depended on him to be elevated to this status in the presence of these elegant people in their pristine world of beauty and exquisiteness.

Yet he kept his mouth shut like a well-trained dog on a hunt because he was after something, he needed something from her, and one outburst of pride, he knew all too well, would cost him the whole shebang, everything he had worked so hard for. She was a means to his end, and although he had never admitted it to himself (consciously at least), he recognized it deep down. He needed her love, her affection—her touch—all because he had burned so many bridges at home. And for some reason he thought that she would never turn on him, that somehow because she existed outside of his day-to-day world and his practical humdrum rhythm of life that it would all be totally different here. What right did she have to be angry with him when he had gone to such great lengths to be with her and to lavish her with gifts and affection and his undivided attention, which perhaps was the greatest sacrifice of all?

But still something was lacking, and suddenly as he paced feverishly along the Malecón, the puzzle pieces were beginning to come together. Jim took a seat on a nearby park bench and hung his head between his knees as he caught his breath. He thought of his life and all of the failed relationships and the fallouts, both romantically and otherwise, and it dawned on him in this desperate moment how truly alone he was. He was alone, so very alone, and it wasn't the world's fault or bad timing or serendipity, where he had long and squarely placed the blame. He was alone because he had used people, all of them—personally, in business, intellectually, even recreation-ally—as a means to an end, rather than as an end in and of themselves.

His gut ached as he sat doubled over, feeling the shame of this realization wash over him and the heavy cost of the life he had chosen for himself. Hot tears welled up in his eyes, and as much as he fought them, he could see them splashing down into the dust beneath him, one by one like little fallen soldiers rushing into a battle they could never win. He had been taught to never cry, that men don't cry and that crying is for little babies and for women and for weak people who live their whole lives controlled and dominated by their emotions rather than by reason and good, sound common sense.

He wiped and fought and wiped some more before he finally gave up and surrendered to the tears, the hot purging taking place in the depths of his soul. He hated the feeling, absolutely hated it with all of his being, because he felt out of control, and Jim Hamilton was never out of control. As he wept and his body convulsed under the pressure of the sobs that were rolling over him in wave after wave, Jim realized that it was control itself that lay at the very root of all of his relational setbacks.

He usually had the means to do whatever he wanted, whenever he wanted, and when he didn't have it, he worked like a dog and pulled strings and cut corners and did whatever it took to get what he wanted. But when it came to people, he could not force them to go along with his plans or to love him or even to like him, so he had always settled for the next best thing— using his eloquence and his affluence and his Southern charm to influence those around him to support his endeavors and to come to his parties and his events and to join his campaign, and in the case of his wife, to join his family.

Yet he knew now in this moment of clarity that it was never

about them, it had never been, about valuing people for their unique gifts and talents and personality, caring for them and their circumstances and what they might be going through at any given time. It was all about Jim—Jim's career and Jim's life and Jim's family. Even his own children had received the brunt of it, all their lives really, being showered with affirmation and praise and rewards when they were performing and making a good name for him and the family, and conversely facing humiliating passive aggression and demeaning outright aggression and worst of all, dad's look of utter disdain and disapproval that he shot across the dining room table whenever report cards came back less than par or sport performances were unimpressive. Conditional approval was the only affection they knew from him, so they strove and strove, just like (he could see now in this moment) he had done as a child and probably his father and his grandfather in their time.

Suddenly and almost involuntarily, Jim cried out, as if the mounting pressure of this revelation had become too much to hold in, and he released a guttural yell, a heart wrenching sound of anguish that would have been frightening for anyone in the general vicinity at such a late hour of night. Fortunately, there was not a soul in the park where he sat, and the cry and the tears remained only with Jim, like a dividend of the path he had chosen to travel many, many years ago. Yet somehow the cry worked, and he was amazed at how good it felt to yell at the top of his lungs, so he did it again, this time with slightly more reservation but still good and loud and authentic. The pressure in his chest began to dissipate just a bit through this new outlet, and one final time, he let out a mighty yell from the core of his being.

No sooner had he closed his mouth than he suddenly became overwhelmed with a deep rolling laughter which quickly encompassed his entire body. At first, he tried to stifle the laughter just as he had with the tears for fear that someone might hear him and think he was a total nut job, but he quickly realized that this explosion of joy could not be contained any more than the tears could. Intellectually, he could no more figure out why he was laughing than why he had just balled his eyes out, but it felt good to laugh and he gave in to its giddy ebb and flow, a rhythm which seemed to sync him simultaneously with his own heart as well as with the natural world around him. The laughter did not last long, but it made him pick up his head and it flushed his cheeks and it stopped the flow of tears that he thought at one point may never end.

But all things have a beginning and an end, and suddenly Jim felt that he was at the end, at the end of himself, at the end of a long road of living life as he always had and at the beginning of—well, he didn't know what he has at the beginning of yet, just a new season of some sort. He lay back and slouched down into the park bench and began to look around for the first time since he had sat down there several minutes prior. To his amazement, he found himself at the park surrounding La Marina Lighthouse, just one hundred yards or so from the base.

Could I have possibly walked all that way? Jim pondered as he looked around in disbelief. The lighthouse was a good three mile walk from la Playa Barranquito where he had started.

Normally that distance would have taken him a full hour to cover at his regular pace, but Jim felt like he had only been gone for 20 or 30 minutes at the most. He rose from his seat, still reeling and second guessing how he had ended up there, and he began to survey his surroundings.

Across the park through the humid night air, a small sliver of light twinkling at the base of the lighthouse caught his eye. As he began to move in that direction, he could see that the door to the tower was once again cracked, and that the light from inside was shining out in a vertical line against the black paint of the door and the frame and against the vast darkness all around stretching out over the massive expanse of ocean which lapped perpetually against the shore just behind it.

IX

His cheeks still flushed from crying and laughing and yelling almost all at the same time, Jim approached the familiar door and stopped dead in his tracks. In his life, to go back, to recant was a sign of weakness and something he vowed never to do except when dictated by absolute necessity. It was what had made him such a strong leader throughout the years. Once he made a decision, he never wavered for any reason. Yet now he could see how this strength, the power of his resolve, had actually become his greatest weakness and a deadly hindrance to the most valuable and precious component of his life—the relationships and people he loved the most. He had burned so many bridges that he felt it would be impossible to go back even if he wanted to, but something in his gut drew him to the light and his hand reached out to take the doorknob.

Perhaps, the carabao will be more forgiving and under-standing than all the people I've hurt over the years, Jim mused, and the very moment he thought it, he knew it was a certainty. He had no way of telling if the strange animal would be at the top of those stairs or if it would ever appear to him again, yet somehow he knew in his heart that he had its forgiveness.

He swung the door open and slipped in, leaving it slightly ajar behind him as before. The light in the tower seemed brighter than last time, perhaps in contrast to the darkness outside, and he could see the gloss on the immaculate navy blue spiral staircase which must have been recently painted. He climbed the stairs slowly and intentionally, thinking of what he would say when he reached the top if the carabao graced him with its presence and trying not to anticipate the weight of disappointment that he would feel if not.

Before he knew it, he stood before the second door at the top of the tower, and again he paused, taking a moment to catch his breath. He bowed his head as if to pray, yet the only words that came out of his mouth were, "Please, please." He whispered so low that he could barely hear his own voice, but something deep down told him that these small words cast into the night air had power. He grabbed the doorknob and twisted and pushed at the same time, and he came spilling into the lantern room like a baby deer learning to find its feet underneath itself.

The room stood silent except for the faint whirring of the lantern rotating methodically inside of the giant lens. The light shone exponentially brighter in the darkness than it had during the daytime, and rather than shielding his face from the sun as he had on his first visit, Jim instinctively covered his eyes from the brightness of the lantern. The pattern of light flashed three times every 15 seconds, which made it even more difficult to look at than a steady light source, because it was constantly causing his pupils to dilate and then to restrict in rapid succession. Jim immediately looked away, shifting his glance out over the dark and endless ocean which looked like a vast, untamed wilderness under the veil of night.

Jim crossed the room to stand before the storm panes on the far side from the door, leaving the flashing light at his back where it was much less bothersome. For a long time, he stood there looking out over the Pacific marveling at its enormity and trying to cherish the unique opportunity to admire it from such a high vantage point. He wondered what it would have been like to be a lighthouse keeper in the days before electric lights replaced lanterns as the optic inside the lens. His life was so far removed from the isolated, remote existence of a keeper that he wondered if he would survive for a week or even a single day. Yet as he stood there in the perfect silence of the tower, he thought that the peace and quiet sure must be nice.

Jim was enjoying himself so much that he almost forgot why he had climbed to the top of the lighthouse in the first place and the hopeful expectation he had carried with him up all those many stairs. He swung his head away from the window and began to peek around the lens against the blinding light which flashed in his face like a spotlight on a one man show. He did not see anything in the dark corners of the room, so he encircled the lens the whole way around just to be sure.

He looked back out over the ocean and shrugged his shoulders as he let out a sigh, realizing in that moment how much he had longed to see the carabao again. For one, he was alone in a foreign country, and moreover, he wanted a chance to apologize for his explosion at their first meeting. He thought it was strange to want to apologize to an animal (or for Jim to want to apologize to anyone or anything at all), but he knew he needed to own up to his anger and frustration in order to make things right, to the carabao and to a whole laundry list of others.

He stood for a moment in silence simultaneously averting his eyes from the flashing light and straining them against the darkness to see if he might detect any motion around him. After several minutes, though, Jim grew tired of waiting and sauntered back toward the door leading to the stairwell.

"You wouldn't have made much of a lighthouse keeper, Jim," he heard a voice from behind him shatter the silence. "Not enough patience."

Jim spun around sharply to find the great carabao standing before him in precisely the same spot where he had appeared before. Its features were much harder to make out in the darkness, but he could see the gray outline of its wide nose and backward facing horns. Its eyes glowed and glistened through the darkness like firelight, and its gaze burned into his soul even more fiercely than before.

Once again facing the lens, Jim braced for the blinding flash of light to hit his tired eyes, but it never came. Puzzled, he waited for a few more seconds until the great creature again broke the silence.

"Jim, if you have not noticed by now, the realm that I inhabit is outside of what you call 'time.' When you are with me, you do not need to count the moments that pass as you do constantly in your world. Here, you can simply be. You may also notice that there is no such thing as worry or anxiety here. These things are produced by your earthly concept of time, and they are rooted in fear. There is no fear here, no running out of time, therefore worry has no place—only perfect peace."

Jim had certainly felt the peace before, with every single encounter. It was impossible to miss. But he did not know the source of it. Now he could see how the sense of timelessness actually produced it. The best way he could describe the feeling was like a weekend that never ended, with no Monday to follow, no appointments or meetings or schedules to draw him out of the joy and tranquility of the present moment.

"So, does that mean I don't have to worry about that pesky light shining in my face?" Jim said with a smirk.

"For now, as long as I am with you," the carabao replied in its calm and even tone. "But when I leave, you're on your own, pal."

Jim smiled at the remark. He allowed a moment to pass and looked down at the floor as he became intensely aware of his need to make amends for his blowup the last time he had stood in this exact spot. It was like his conscience had kicked into high gear, and he could not think of a single other thing if he tried—his thoughts were completely clouded by the shouting necessity to seek forgiveness. It wasn't a thought so much as a compulsion, something he knew in his heart that he must do and that he could somehow visualize himself doing, like a strange impression lingering in his mind's eye.

He was comforted by the carabao's gentle voice and felt no animosity exuding from it. He thought about what state he would be in if the tables had been turned and how he would be burning up with anger and bitter rage if someone had spoken to him the same way he had spoken to it, particularly so recently. He knew deep down that his premonition was correct, that he had already been forgiven, yet for some reason, now that the moment was upon him and he was faced with the reality of swallowing his pride and admitting that he had done something wrong, he froze up and was unable to speak. He tried feebly to express his remorse, but only a thin rasp emerged from his throat and he could not manage to produce a single syllable, much less vocalize his full sentiments. He stood frozen like a statue with his mouth gaping for a few moments before the carabao had mercy on him and interrupted his floundering.

"Why did you come back, Jim?"

"I—I," the block in Jim's larynx felt like a steel trap enclosed around his neck and chest with such great force that he feared his breathing may be stifled if it carried on any longer. He had a sudden awareness that he must tell the truth, that the key to unlock the torrent of words and emotions and regret that he felt at the moment was unfiltered, brutal honesty.

Jim painfully cleared his throat. "I had a falling out," he began, each word coating his rasped gullet like honey. "And I realized that I'm all alone. And, and it's nobody's fault but mine. I have been so—so cruel. And I have burned so many bridges. You saw it, I have devoured the people in my life with my words and even more with my harsh resolve and sort of unwavering, drill sergeant-like intensity. I have been so concerned with being right and maintaining the upper hand in all of my relationships that, well, I don't have any relationships left at all. Not any real ones, nothing healthy or life-giving. Just rubble, the rubble of a life crumbling under the weight of one man's selfish desire to climb to the top no matter who he had to step on and run over to get there."

Jim's words flowed out of him like a waterfall spilling over a dam, immediately releasing the built up tension he had felt just moments prior. It was the same revelation he had received on the park bench less than an hour ago, but to speak it aloud, to share it with another being somehow cemented it into reality. And now Jim felt that he owned it in a way that was much more real and tangible than when it was just a thought milling around in his head.

"Jim, you're speaking in the third person," the carabao responded with a twinkle in its eye. "I assume you're talking about yourself?"

This little speck of wit eased the tension and made Jim chuckle to himself just enough to provide a temporary respite for his weary, introspective soul. He was a politician, of course he spoke in the third person from time to time. It came with the territory. He reflected in that moment, *Humor is perhaps the best sign of true forgiveness.*

"And speaking of forgiveness," the great creature interrupted his train of thought. "I forgive you. For the record, you didn't actually apologize, but I'm willing to let bygones be bygones."

This time Jim laughed audibly as the carabao's banter washed over him like a healing salve. Immediately, it lifted the heavy weight of the atmosphere in the room, but even more so, Jim knew that the bridge between them had been fully repaired. The forgiveness that had been extended to him was not given begrudgingly or with any reservations whatsoever. He could feel that there was not even a tiny hint of bitterness or resentment lingering toward him. He and the carabao, and the Great Spirit behind it, had a completely blank slate to begin anew.

"Well, thank you," Jim responded after a brief moment of silence. "And *for the record*, I am sorry that I blew up at you. I take it back."

"Again, you are forgiven."

"Please, tell me your name. I don't think I ever got it the first time." Jim's tone and overall attitude toward the majestic creature had shifted dramatically and carried a radically different quality now than it had before—much different than with all of the other spirit animals he had encountered—and he could feel it tangibly, like a softness in his heart. It reminded him of the difference between having lunch with an acquaintance from work and sitting down to dinner with an old friend.

"My name is Aguinaldo. How much do you know, Jim, about the Philippine–American War?"

"Well," Jim replied, pausing for a moment to think. "I know

that it directly followed the Spanish-American War and that whoever named both of those wars didn't have a creative bone in their body." He grinned and then continued. "But it was a war between America and the Spanish colony of the Philippines, which the United States purchased from Spain, and that's about all I know. Oh, and that America won."

"Close, but not quite," Aguinaldo responded gently. "It was a war between the United States and the First Philippine Republic. You see, the Filipino people had already declared independence from Spain when America bought it in December of 1898. How exactly does a nation go about purchasing another sovereign nation?"

"Well, that's not totally fair," Jim rebutted. "The Philippines were a colony of Spain for just shy of 350 years. How can they just declare independence and become a sovereign nation all of a sudden, conveniently right before they were sold to the US?"

"How did the United States declare independence from Britain and become a sovereign nation?"

"Ok, good point. We outmaneuvered those redcoats and gave 'em what they had coming to 'em."

At this, the carabao snorted producing a semblance of laughter which echoed through the lantern room resembling a cross between a whinny and a bray. "Yes, Jim. Whatever you just said. So what was the difference between the Philippine Revolution and the American Revolution? The Filipinos outmaneuvered the Spanish and gave 'em what they had coming to 'em, as you so eloquently put it. But why didn't they have the same result as the Americans?"

Jim lifted his hand to his chin and rested two fingers over his mouth as he pondered the question for a short time before responding. "I suppose," he began a little more cautiously, "that they routed their enemy on one side and were met by an even stronger one on the other."

"Precisely, and what exactly was the difference between the Americans who conquered them at the turn of the 20th century and the Spanish conquistadors who conquered them in the 16th century?"

"Everything. I mean, the ideology couldn't be more different. The Spanish were an empire seeking to dominate lands and people groups to establish colonies that would divert wealth and natural resources and human capital back to the motherland. The United States promotes freedom and democracy all over the world. The Filipinos weren't strong enough to govern themselves, and everyone knew it."

"And the British Colonies in North America were? What gives someone the right to self govern? Is it strength of might or strength of resolve? Why would the Filipino people deserve any less of a chance than the American people to govern themselves?"

Jim ran his thumb back and forth underneath his lower jaw and looked out over the vast expanse of the Pacific as he chewed on this series of questions. He felt no rush to answer, so he stood in silence for a few moments and strained to make out the thin line where the dark water met the even darker cloak of night enveloping the landscape as far as the eye could see.

Freedom and democracy were the ideals that Jim grew up

on like every American kid, his bread and his butter, his base-ball and his endless summers and his ability to pursue his dreams without anyone saying otherwise. To question these was to question his identity, his way of life, what he had fought for and worked so hard for as a legislator for nearly three de-cades now.

"It's just no comparison," Jim replied coolly. "If we hadn't relieved the Philippines from Spanish rule, someone else would have. And it would have been 10 times as brutal. They were bet-ter off under our control, and they got their independence in the end."

"Try telling that to the hundreds of thousands of Filipino citizens who lost their lives through the ravages of war. Try telling that to the children who suddenly had to study English in their schools because it was the language of their new 'own-ers.' Try telling that to a proud people who finally saw the light at the end of the tunnel of centuries of oppressive rule only to see it snuffed out by a nation claiming to be the global bastion of freedom and democracy eight thousand miles away on the other side of this ocean you are mesmerized by."

Jim instantly felt a rage rise up from his belly, but some-thing calmed his temper and he tried to sort out all that had just been thrown at him. Then a question, not an answer, came to his mind that seemed to throw a slight kink in his mental pro-cess up to this point.

Well, why," Jim began again, "did the United States want the Philippines in the first place? What good is it to own, and govern, a bunch of islands on the other side of the world?"

"Ah, now you are asking me questions! If you can tell me the answer to that question, you may end up meeting with the Great Spirit face to face sooner than we all thought. And with that, my friend, I must bid you adieu."

While the words were still echoing through the lantern room, a flash of light hit Jim's eyes, temporarily blinding him and causing him to recoil from his position directly in front of the lens. When he opened his eyes again, splotches of yellow and orange and red slowly faded from his view, and the carabao was nowhere to be found. The lantern had resumed its steady rotation, lighting up the night sky with a steady beam that shot forth like a ray of hope and consolation piercing the fierce darkness that covered the water with an impenetrable blanket of despair and isolation.

Everywhere the light touched, scanning endless stretches of water for miles and miles, it acted as a constant reminder like a faithful messenger that the ships and seafaring men were not alone, that there was a place for them—a port, a home. Someone, somewhere was waiting for them to return safely and soundly, to hug them and to kiss them and to tell them that it was all going to be alright. Someone, somewhere cared.

Jim reminisced and wondered who was out there for him, waiting for him to return, longing for his embrace. *The problem is,* he mulled over to himself, *I have been away so incredibly long. Sure, I have been physically present, but what does that amount to when my heart wasn't in it? My heart—if I even have a heart anymore.*

Jim sat down on the floor and leaned his head back against

the cold, metal wall which supported the massive storm panes above his head. He began to weep once again, but this time selfishly, thinking about his home port and who would be there to greet him when he snuck off the airplane to resume the shell of his former life. He wept because his mom and his dad were both dead, and because he hadn't been much of a dad himself to his children, or a husband to his wife.

He reminisced that hadn't been much of a son before that, watching his mother languishing with Parkinson's in a nursing home and knowing that she would have been better off in his care, with family around to cheer her up and to give her a sense of normalcy in her last years and months. But he was never home, and what sense of normalcy did he have anyway? Besides, it was unfair to place such a heavy burden on his wife and children if he could not share the load.

He cried because he had been belted so severely as a child that he swore he would never spank his own son, although his lack of restraint had made his son reckless, foolhardy and utterly rebellious. His son hated authority, particularly when it came from his dad, and the showdowns had no winners—only losers. His wife lost the most because she felt like she was losing her family and her sanity when they would yell at each other in the house and most recently when Jim had tried unsuccessfully to physically restrain him and blows were thrown and her antique lamp with the blue china dogs on it was smashed to pieces on the floor. It went down in the books as collateral damage, but all collateral has a price tag and when the tab begins to add up, everyone can feel the weight. At least in Jim's house they can, and there are seemingly fewer and fewer moments of respite these days.

It is amazing how different a family can look, Jim thought as he wiped his eyes and nose on the sleeve of his shirt, *on a Sunday morning or when posing for a campaign mailer in front of the governor's mansion—pristine and picture perfect and almost sparkling on the outside—when on the inside they are eaten up with bitterness and hate and layer upon layer of resentment toward one another. It makes it worse really because there you are all together collectively displaying an image that is fake and contrived, and everyone knows it but no one is allowed to say a word. It's like keeping a deep, dark secret with your enemy, and you want with all of your heart to expose him, but in doing so, you would expose yourself as well.*

Jim had always lived on the inside looking out and had finally come to accept the duality of life in his world, embracing the hidden and masked brokenness of his closest relationships as his constant companion, as a way of life. There were no outlets, no one safe enough to confide in, and no point in doing so anyhow. Everyone knew and no one knew at the same time. Everyone felt the sting, yet still everyone felt like they were the only ones. That was the most insidious part of it all. The unspoken passive aggressive code kept everyone isolated and constantly swallowing their deepest and most honest feelings until they festered and grew so bitter that when they did eventually make their way to the surface, they sounded like the worst kind of hate and bigotry you could imagine.

No one grows up wanting to hate another human being, Jim

thought as he continued to stare up at the ceiling of the lantern room. *Especially not for their looks or for the color of their skin or something asinine like that. But hate has a way of building and growing when it's not dealt with, and it has to come out somehow. So it surfaces in the most awful ways, in putrid ways, and people become black haters or white haters or Hispanic haters and that's not what they are at all, that's not where the stick is. The hang up is in their own home, their own community, their own world, but they take it out on another world, a world they don't know anything about and couldn't possibly understand because they have never lived there. But they hate it anyhow because there is a safe distance, and it feels good to have an outlet for the bitterness and resentment to flow, regardless of how misguided the direction.*

Jim was reminded of how he used to take out his rage, the rage he felt toward his father but could never express, on the birds and squirrels in his backyard with his pellet gun and how much he enjoyed watching the fur and feathers fly and the unsuspecting creatures fall to the ground limp and lifeless. He had never asked the question of why, yet suddenly he knew the answer. It was all a mechanism to reroute his anger, the anger he felt over the welts that covered his backside and sometimes his arms and legs, the rage he felt over the word curses that covered his identity with "stupid" and "failure" and "not enough." He took it out on the neighborhood kids and the black men who worked in the lumberyard his dad owned, not with force but with his cutting wit and the power of demeaning and hateful words wielded at just the right time. He took it out on his own wife and children, his office staff and colleagues, slowly and steadily debasing the world around him so he could slowly but surely rise to the top.

I have been so cruel. So, so cruel. Jim didn't have any tears left to cry but his eyes and cheeks were still moist from the deluge, so he wiped them one final time with the shirtsleeve that was still dry and slowly clamored to his feet, holding onto the black railing located just above his head which ran around the perimeter of the lantern room. Once he had his feet back underneath him, he resumed his gaze out over the dark and empty ocean, being careful to avert his eyes from making direct contact with the beam of the lens. *I am no different*, Jim thought, *than this darkness. A void of light and love and everything. Please, help me.*

He didn't know who this thought was directed to, but he knew that someone or something was still there with him. He turned to leave the room and felt a wisp of air breeze across the back of his neck, a small eddy of movement in the atmosphere above him, just enough to be perceptible.

"Thank you," Jim whispered out loud. He opened the heavy door and bolted down the lighthouse steps, whistling the whole way down.

X

As Jim started down the Malecón back toward the villa, he wondered what Aguinaldo had meant when he said that Jim would meet with the Great Spirit face to face. And sooner than he thought. *Aren't they all the same? Didn't I already meet with him four times over? How can a spirit have a face anyhow?*

Jim's mind fluttered between replaying the conversation he had just finished and dreading the reception he would get when he met with his *mistress* face to face. She had always been very forgiving in the past, which was one reason why he loved her so much, but you never could tell with a fiery Peruvian. She could be sweet one minute and erupt the next into an explosion of colloquial Spanish that he had never heard in any class he had ever taken. So he decided that he would just have to tread cautiously.

As he walked, Jim continued to glance up and out over the Pacific where he could see the beam from La Marina Lighthouse—flash, pause, flash, flash, and then repeat. Slowly, the beam grew smaller and smaller until it was only a blip in his periphery, then the path turned inland and he could see it no longer.

He thought as he walked of a story he read in college about an infamous pirate who was captured and brought face to face with Alexander the Great, who ruled the majority of the known world at that time. Alexander the Great grilled the hardened criminal with a furrow in his brow and fire in his eyes. "How dare you molest the seas?" he asked him. Without hesitation, the pirate looked back at him and replied, "How dare you molest the whole world? Because I do it with a small boat, I am called a pirate and a thief. You, with a great navy, molest the world and are called an emperor."

What did the United States want with a nation of war-torn islands all the way on the other side of the Pacific?

Jim had always been an avid student of history, yet he was coming to realize that there were gaps in his thinking—not so much the what or the how, but the why, the motivation and often hidden agendas behind the events that have shaped human history and subsequently the world he found himself in. Jim had long ago come to the conclusion that if human beings could screw something up, they would—and with flying colors. For him, the saddest part about studying history was seeing how things could have taken a slightly different turn—if the powers to be had listened to this voice instead of that voice or if they had taken the time to think through the long term ramifications of their actions—how night and day the outcomes could have been and how much better off the world would be today as a result. But he also recognized that the world is full of hindsight history majors and determined that what the world needs is solution makers, not rearview mirror know-it-alls.

He thought of the annexation of Hawaii, an area of history he knew a whole lot more about than the acquisition of the Philippines, which happened interestingly enough the same year that the United States purchased the Philippines from Spain in 1898. Five years prior in 1893, a group of businessmen living on the islands overthrew the sovereign Kingdom of Hawaii, with the help of a convenient cameo by 162 United States marines. The next year, Sanford Dole became the self-proclaimed president of the newly formed Republic of Hawaii, and five years after that in 1899, his cousin James Dole founded the pineapple company that would later become Dole Food Company, the largest producer of fruits and vegetables in the world today.

Guess it can't hurt your start-up to have 1.75 million acres of land seized from the royal family at your disposal, Jim thought as he revisited this chapter of American history with a new lens.

Jim found it interesting that the guy who overthrew and replaced the queen of Hawaii (and whose new government sentenced her to five years of hard labor, which she did not do) was not the one whose name we remember today. But he paved the way for it all to happen, for Dole to be the iconic symbol on the fruit cups and juice boxes that Jim so fondly remembered from his childhood. Then it hit him why the United States would fight a bloody war all the way across an ocean for those thousands of little islands called the Philippines.

They were making a way—a *way for business domination, a way for cultural domination. They would never realize it in their day, but to rule the Pacific with trade routes and refueling stations was only the next step in something so much larger— Manifest Destiny.*

Yet how ironic, Jim pondered as his mood suddenly shifted from jovial to sullen, *that the culture of freedom and democracy now seemed so, well, forceful and undemocratic— soldiers and an unelected president, no diplomacy, no vote, just brute force. Isn't that the way the world is though? And the way it will always be?*

In the flow of his trance-like train of thought, Jim did not even notice that he had arrived back in Barranco, back to his lover's villa, back to face the music. He walked the final 100 feet or so with a somber air of negative anticipation, the kind of feeling that some heavy object might be thrown at your head at any minute and you would know that it was completely justif-ied. This was mingled with the sinking feeling that the object of his present meditation had produced deep down inside of him, a feeling of abject horror at the way the world goes 'round mixed with a feeling of utter powerlessness to do anything about it.

Jim walked into the front room of the apartment slowly and cautiously, like a wild animal in the headlights ready to dart at any moment. He honestly did not know what to expect and had been on such an emotional rollercoaster already, he wasn't sure that he had the mental and spiritual energy left to regulate his emotions in the case of a flare up. But he had nowhere else to go, and besides, he truly yearned to make amends and move on from the anger and the outbursts and the manipulation that had led him to the place of isolation, the lonely island where he had been living for far too long.

Thick, hanging silence engulfed him as he crept through the room, and he wondered what time it was anyhow. In his hot-headed dash out earlier, Jim had left his phone on the charger in the kitchen and had noticed himself feeling quite naked without it, unable to check on whatever it was that was so important for him to check on. In the end, it had served him well, but it had left him unable to keep track of the time, which was probably another blessing in disguise.

Jim had almost made it across the room to the couch where he figured he could crash for the remainder of the night when he hit a creaky floorboard which instantly filled the room with a thunderous sound. *Creak*, it shouted as his foot pressed down on the hardwood, and *creak*, it moaned again as the weight of his body lifted from the slightly loose slat. Jim stopped dead in his tracks, hunching his shoulders forward and clenching his teeth like he had been caught in a bank vault with the loot. He looked intensely guilty without meaning to for a few moments as he listened ferociously for a reciprocating response from somewhere else in the house. After he decided that he had waited long enough and that he was most likely in the clear, he tiptoed his next step like a bandit when, piercing the silence, a shrill sound rang out from the bedroom.

"Jim?! By God, I hope it's you. Jim?! Jim?!"

He could hear footsteps scampering across the floor, and within moments, his mistress appeared from around the corner, still wrapping herself in her light pink bathrobe, awkwardly fumbling with the sash to make a knot of some kind as she caught sight of him for the first time since their spat earlier in the evening.

"Oh, Jim! Alabado sea Dios!" she exclaimed as she flung herself at him and threw her arms around his shoulders. Not a moment later, she recoiled back one half step and slapped him across the face with a motion so swift that Jim never saw her hand rise or fall. "You cretino! You scared me near to my death!"

Jim stood motionless, stunned from the commotion and the

suddenness of the whole interaction and the fire he could feel beginning to creep across the whole left side of his face. Somehow, he regained his senses as he lifted his hand to his cheek, and he knew he had to say something so he said the first thing that came to mind.

"I'm sorry. I'm just so very sorry. I'm sorry that—"

Jim would have gone on apologizing for who knows how long if she hadn't cut him off with a kiss that hit him with about as much impact and force as her palm had just moments prior. He sank into the redemption of her kiss and of her embrace as the enveloping warmth of the moment made his mind go blank. When he came to, he was lying next to her in bed, and she was fast asleep.

The morning light crept in horizontally through the blinds projecting a striped pattern of dark and light on the aqua blue down comforter which halfway covered them both. Jim rolled onto his back, lay his head squarely on the center of his pillow and stared at the ceiling fan going around and around, mechanically just like the light atop La Marina Lighthouse, and he closed his eyes as he drifted back off to sleep.

XI

An icy cold sensation crept up Jim's neck as he stared hard into the blackest, most enveloping darkness he had ever experienced. He strained his eyes against the thick veil which seemed to hem him in on all sides, and he could barely make out a sliver of light maybe 30 yards ahead of him. As he continued to fix his eyes on this single focal point, he could begin to see the faint undulating of waves cresting and falling, cresting and falling on either side of him. He could feel the hard fiberglass of the boat's hull pressing against his chest and up under his armpits as he leaned his head out over the edge of the dinghy to track the splotch of light which seemed to be growing closer and closer with each passing moment.

The boat drifted on and on, and suddenly Jim could make out arms and legs and a head, the outline of a little girl floating atop the water completely motionless—lifeless—her dark hair flowing back and forth in sync with the movement of the water. Just seconds before the body (which Jim did not know was dead or alive) came within his reach, he heard a blood curdling yell, a noise unlike any he had ever heard in his life.

The scream shocked his senses, and his droopy eyes flew wide open as he became fully alert like he had awoken from a nightmare. For one moment, he could see the face of his daughter, white as a corpse, before it slipped underneath the surface of the menacing water. He lunged forward, stretching himself out as far as humanly possible, as he watched her face and hair disappear one behind the other, being replaced in the same instant by a hand shooting up through the water's surface.

The hand appeared cold and lifeless like the rest of the body, but it stretched and reached and seemed to call for help with every movement of its circular blind groping. Jim extended himself with all of his might and could feel the bitter cold of the water creeping up his arm, but the hand continued to evade his grasp, always just beyond his reach. He began to paddle frantically with both arms to propel the boat forward, but the harder he worked, the lower the hand sunk into the water.

He began to cry out with all of his might, appealing to the hand to push, to bridge the gap, to make the connection. He stopped paddling and reached one final time, the hull of the boat digging into his torso where he balanced, teetering on the verge of falling in himself, as he watched the fingertips slip below the surface of the water, a mere six inches away from his outstretched hand. A sense of complete powerlessness overwhelmed him as he let out a final shriek of despair and utter anguish at the coldhearted, unfeeling water which had just consumed his beloved only daughter. Unable to maintain his teetering perch any longer, he collapsed into the hull of the boat overcome by uncontrollable heaves and sobs that shook him from the core of his being outward to the tips of every extremity.

XII

Jim shot up in his bed covered in sweat. He leaned his head back and grasped his chest with his open palm to catch his breath. His heart raced under the pressure of the pulsing nerves in his electrified hand. It had only been a dream. When the shock lifted and he finally regained his composure, he noticed his phone buzzing and buzzing on the bedside table next to him. Every time it stopped buzzing, there would be a five second pause and then the buzzing would start again. He could not figure out how his phone had gotten there in the first place, since the last place he remembered leaving it was on the charger in the kitchen. Plus, it had been on "Do Not Disturb" since he had arrived at the airport two days prior. But sure enough, it was ringing now, and there seemed to be no end in sight.

He rolled over onto his side and propped himself up on his right forearm as he scooped up the phone with his left hand and brought it before his groggy eyes. His daughter's name populated the screen, and his mind immediately began to race. *Why would she be calling me again and again like this? Something must be wrong. This is not like her.*

Jim looked over to make sure that his mistress was still sound asleep and darted from the bed to take the call in the living room.

"Sweetie," Jim spoke frantically into the phone in a half whisper, trying to get as far away from the bedroom door as possible. "Are you alright? What on earth is going on?"

Images from the dream raced through his head—her lifeless body floating, the cry for help, the hand reaching and searching and then sinking—and his heart began to pound uncontrollably. There was a momentary pause. Jim closed his eyes and held his breath like he was waiting for a guilty verdict from an unfavorable jury.

"It's mom," the voice resounded on the other end of the line. "She had a stroke. We need you here."

There was another pause as shock waves crept up Jim's spine and across his neck and over his head until his entire body felt completely paralyzed from top to bottom.

"I know I'm not supposed to call and interrupt your trip or

whatever, but I'm scared, dad. We're all scared. Please, please just come home."

Jim's mind raced and he could not think and he felt that his lips would not work even if he knew what to say, but again he knew that he must act and that this was his time to be brave and if there was one thing Jim Hamilton was not, it was a coward.

"I will be on the first flight home, honey," Jim managed to eke out of his nearly paralyzed lips.

Silence flooded Jim's world for what seemed like an eternity and was eventually broken by the sound of muffled sobs on the other end.

"Ok, dad," he heard over the rise and fall of heaving breaths. "I gotta go."

The connection ended, and Jim sat staring at the little screen in his hand, hating his phone and technology and this world where you cannot escape anywhere you go. Yet more than anything, he hated himself in that moment for *wanting* to escape, for *wanting* to run away—from his problems, from his family, from his life—rather than to face it all head on like a man.

He gritted his teeth and began to frantically gather all of his things like a madman, and he flew out the door of the villa as the first rays of morning were creeping over the horizon. He requested an Uber to the airport, but his legs refused to stop walking so he paced frantically in the direction that the car appeared to be coming from.

The next seven minutes seemed like an eternity—stalled, waiting, no progress—but once he was in the car on his way to the airport, he felt much better. He was moving forward, no longer stuck. He felt that it was true of a whole lot more than just a taxi ride. He felt unstuck for the first time in a long time, and he didn't know what he would share with his daughter and the rest of his family when he arrived, but he knew there was something deep down in his heart for them now, something to impart to them, where there had only been a gaping void for so long.

As Jim watched the murals and brightly colored cafés and shops of Barranco zip by his window for the second time that week, he mourned over the shortness of his trip. Yet time did not seem to have the same hold on him as it did before, and he let out a long sigh as he leaned his head against the car window thinking of all that had transpired in the matter of a couple of days.

As the car approached the airport, Jim fished around in his bag looking for his watch, which he had taken off the night before, but immediately his eye caught a flash of red and he pulled out the ball cap he had bought on his way to Lima. *Make America Great Again.* The hat had not grown on him during the trip, but necessity bound him to it, so he dutifully put it on.

Before the car had even come to a complete stop in front of the main terminal, Jim sprang into high gear, grabbing his bag and vaulting out of the car to see how early he could get on a flight. Once inside, he balked at the size of the lines at both airlines offering direct flights home, and he picked what he thought looked like the shortest of the two.

Only suckers stand in these lines, he thought as impatient rage flushed his checks, *now I'm one of them.*

As Jim stood in line, he analyzed and judged every single person in front of him who was keeping him from moving forward with his trip and his life. *Too many bags, too fat, too colorful, too tacky, too much PDA.* He pronounced sentences bitterly in his mind one by one until he had covered everyone, and then he started over again. The line appeared to be at a complete standstill, and just as he was reaching into his pocket for his phone to call the airline, the ground shook violently all around him, and Jim fell to the floor clumsily, spilling over his bag which had been planted next to his right foot.

Jim closed his eyes instinctively during the fall, and when he reopened them, he was surprised to see that he was the only one on the floor. Immediately, he heard a familiar voice behind him.

"Hurry up and wait, isn't it always, Jim?" the voice rang out.

Jim whipped his head around to pinpoint where the voice had come from, and standing before him in the aisle next to the line towered the great and majestic form of Tatanka. Before he had time to gather his thoughts, the massive animal spoke again.

"Tell me how you really feel about those people? Have you ever stopped for a moment, just a single moment, to consider someone else's life circumstances? Have you learned nothing from our interactions thus far?"

"Just tell me, please," Jim began nearly breathless from the sudden jolt that had brought him to the ground, "that time is stopped. I have to get home right away." Jim looked up at the bison with a fierceness in his eyes like a caged animal.

"Oh, give it a rest, Jim," Tatanka replied sternly. "You get one phone call and now all of a sudden you're mister family man? You could care less about your wife, or why would you be here cheating on her? The only reason you are racing home like a frenetic madman is because you were jolted by the dream that the Great Spirit gave you about your daughter. You love her more than your wife, and this is more about her than anyone else. Deep down, you don't even really care if your wife lives or dies."

Jim sat stunned as the words pressed down on him like a heavy weight crushing his entire body underneath a waterfall of unbridled conviction, guilt and shame. His first thought when he had received the phone call that morning was one of relief that it was his wife and not his daughter in the hospital in critical condition. His second thought had been that if his wife died, he could marry his mistress legitimately. Sadness blanketed his soul as he came face to face with the wickedness of his own thought-life.

Yet the very next moment, a violent rage rose up from deep within him, a sense of righteous indignation that overtook his mind and overwhelmed his emotions in a flash. Jim hopped to his feet and flew at the enormous animal who stood placidly before him, shouting with fists clenched in hatred and anger.

"How can you sit there and read my thoughts and intrude on my most private space and look so innocent like it's nothing at all, like this isn't all your doing? You probably gave my wife that stroke. You probably want her to die more than I do—and me too for that matter!"

Jim stared with hatred in his heart into the gentle yet fierce eyes of Tatanka, the majestic spirit animal who had intercepted him only a few days prior and who had spun his whole life out of control. He did not flinch or budge although he suddenly became aware of the fact that he was outmatched in every way, particularly physically. Yet nothing in the world could have made him stand down in that moment, except a heart attack which he feared since he didn't see how his heart could possibly beat any faster than it already was.

"Jim," Tatanka began with an eerie coolness. "The Great Spirit is not the author of disease, death and destruction. Humanity has brought that upon herself. There is a great enemy in this world, but it is not external as you have always imagined—your great enemy lurks inside your very own heart. The Great Spirit did not cause the events of this day, but he has orchestrated them to reveal something very wicked at the core of your being. Jim, your thoughts this morning were not natural, nor are they acceptable in the great order of things. We have seen this inside of you, and out of the infinite mercy of the Great Spirit, we have now allowed you to see it as well.

"True love is unconditional," Tatanka continued, "but it never recognizes a fatal flaw in someone else and turns its back. When you see a loved one spiraling out of control, a real friend doesn't sweep it under the rug—they intervene. True love always accepts others as they are, but it must also spur them on to greatness—or else it is not love at all. Jim, you cannot be great with wickedness running unchecked in your heart. You must decide. You must choose whether you will continue to harbor this wickedness and let it drive you to anger, or if you will let it go and allow the Great Spirit to lead you into a life of peace and love."

Jim turned sharply away from the great beast and stormed off several paces before a thought stopped him dead in his tracks. He had been turning and running, turning and running for so long—from conflict, from accountability, from discomfort or tension with anyone—and every time, every encounter, it grew more and more pronounced, more and more violent. His movements were sharper and more flagrant, but what froze him was the sudden realization that his anger had become so rigid and so defined that he could no longer control it. Suddenly in that moment, he could see that it was controlling him.

Slowly, he turned on his heels and reluctantly lifted his head to look Tatanka in the eyes. He could see the fire flickering and burning in those two glowing orbs, the fire of passion and the fire of love. Jim licked his lips and rubbed his tongue against the back of his teeth as he swallowed his pride like a schoolboy who had run away from home only to return with his tail between his legs.

"What, exactly, do you want from me?" Jim spoke slowly and deliberately.

"It's not what I want *from* you, Jim," Tatanka replied without fluctuation in his countenance and maintaining his same gentle tone of voice. "It's what I want *for* you. I want to help you, *we* want to help you—to fulfill your destiny on this earth, your destiny as a legislator of your people, as a chief, and as a husband and a father. You are so used to taking that you have forgotten how to give, or even to receive for that matter. You have become so cautious of others and so callous because you think everyone in this world operates like you do, like a mercenary, but it's not true.

"There are many today," Tatanka went on, "who are still partnered with the Great Spirit to bring goodness and kindness and love to this world and to their fellow man. You work among some of them, but sadly so many in your nation have turned away from selfless service to pursue wealth and notoriety and individual gain of one sort or another. But you, Jim, have a pure heart. We have seen it, and despite your many flaws and poor decisions, we know the potential you carry to bring forth great good and to undo much of the evil that has permeated your culture and saturated your people through greed and selfish ambition.

"But," the great buffalo's tone suddenly grew stern, "you must trust us. You have wavered up to this point, back and forth and back and forth, but now time is of the essence. You have used up all nine of your lives, Jim, and you have none left. You must choose to jump in headfirst and trust this process or else you will not be afforded another opportunity. You have been chosen, but you must choose back or else the Great Spirit will find someone else to partner with him. Your time is now, Jim—what do you say?"

Beads of sweat had been collecting on Jim's forehead as the massive animal spoke, and now they were joining together and racing down the sides of his face like falling stars, dropping to the ground off both edges of his jaw and landing on the hard tile floor below. He could feel the intensity in the atmosphere pressing down on him like a lead blanket, weighing on every fiber of his being. He wanted to believe in this fantastic creature who stood before him, in the process, in the—Great Spirit—but something deep inside was resisting, fighting tooth and nail, screaming at him to hold onto the Jim Hamilton he had spent so many years grooming and developing, the Jim Hamilton who had a brilliant future of unparalleled success and greatness ahead of him, the Jim Hamilton who would one day run for president.

Yet the very thought of running for president, which had driven him like a madman through the unbearable and untenable seasons, suddenly began to deflate in his heart like a balloon with a slow leak. *What good is it to be the leader of the free world if you are controlled by anger and disdain for others? What good is it to be a husband and a father if all you care about is yourself?*

Instantly, the other half of the levee that had broken at the park bench along the Malecón—where Jim had wept for himself and for being all alone in this world—came toppling down as the first truly selfless thought Jim had harbored in three decades rushed down into the canals of his soul like an unstoppable, rushing torrent. He had been broken on that park bench because, for the first time in as long as he could remember, he connected with his own pain and misery and isolation.

This time, though, the cracks and fissures penetrated to a place unfathomably deeper, splaying open the very core of his being as he could feel the pain and the anguish and the utter heartache he had inflicted on others throughout a lifetime of relentless self-striving—and the soul crushing effect felt a hundred times more intense, like standing under Niagara Falls at high season. Sobs shook his whole body as Jim Hamilton collapsed onto the floor in a puddle of tears and sweat.

XIII

For what seemed like an eternity, Jim wept. He cried for himself, for how blind he had been and for all the time he had wasted stepping over others to make a name for himself. He cried for his wife, for his utter lack of tenderness and love. He cried for his children, for how they had grown up learning more about him from the papers than from his time at home with them. He cried for the moments he had missed along the way—not selfishly, not for the opportunity he had lost, but for the void he had created—in his son's heart never making it to his games, in his daughter's life never being there to hear the secrets of her heart, and in his marriage for treating his wife more like a personal assistant than a lover and a friend.

All his life, Jim had been taught not to cry, that boys don't cry because girls cried enough tears for the both of them and that little boys who cried like wimps were easy targets. But by now he did not care one lick about all that nonsense, and he knew it was not true anyhow. Plus, he could not have stopped the river of salty tears if he had tried with all his might, nor did he want to. There was something therapeutic about it that he simply could not describe. Here he was in this pathetic, vulnerable state on a dirty public floor pouring his heart out to nobody with this strange creature looking on at the whole thing probably thinking he was the most unkempt politician to ever walk the face of planet earth, yet there was some great release at the very same time that washed over him, lifting the heavy burden of life off his shoulders—and it felt good.

Jim did not realize how intensely the affair had been weighing on him until he could feel it too lift. Keeping secrets is hard work, much harder than telling the truth, and suddenly Jim knew that the jig was up. He had to come clean. He could not wait. He had to get out from under the weight of lies and deception that started as fun and games and had become a terror, haunting him day and night. It's why he had bought that stupid hat in the first place trying to hide—and from who? He was the governor of Georgia for heaven's sake. There was no hiding nor did Jim have any inclination to do so at this moment. It was going to be painful, but he would come clean and beg for mercy and grace and forgiveness, fully aware that he might not receive any of those things. But it was the right thing to do— the only thing to do—so Jim set his face toward the moment when he would let his cards down and face the music for his actions.

"Jim," Tatanka's voice echoed through his consciousness, startling him out of his introspective stupor.

Jim felt a small shudder move across his head and shoulders, and he looked up abruptly. "Can't you tell I'm having a moment," he said, staring the great beast directly in its eyes and wiping away tears and snot with his shirt sleeve at the same time. Suddenly, he burst out laughing and nearly fell backward onto the hard tile floor. He realized that all of those tears and all of that crying had been paving the way for something, for this outburst of happiness and lightness and joy, and that the same muscles he had used to weep were the same muscles now engaged in deep belly laughter. It did not make any sense to him why he was laughing so hysterically now or why he had been consumed with laughter on the park bench by the Malecón, but for several moments, he allowed the wave to completely overtake him. It felt awkward because he could not explain it but refreshing in a childish sort of way, like an intense bout of nostalgia or deja vu.

The great beast did not laugh but its eyes twinkled like little diamonds, and it did not break its gaze for a moment. A different quality had descended over Tatanka's face, a new softness that looked like acceptance and love and compassion personified. Jim knew that this animal or spirit or whatever it was understood precisely what was happening to him and that he did not need to say a word in defense or explanation of his rather odd and diametrical outbreaks.

"Jim," Tatanka's voice thundered after giving him a few moments to catch his breath, "there is nothing odd about your laughter or your tears. The only odd thing is how seldom I see true tears and genuine laughter these days. These are dark times, and it pleases me more than you know to see you, well, free.

"You have been bottled up," the great bison continued, "for a very long time completely by your own doing. We have tried to reach you, but in that state, it is very hard to penetrate, even for the Great Spirit. Your selfish ambition has clouded your thinking longer than you realize, long before you ever met your wife or ran for office. What she and those around you mistook for empathy and genuineness was simply your raw passion to overcome the next hurdle, to climb the next mountain, and you needed them by your side to do it.

"You won them over, but the heart connection was lacking because true love is always a two-way street. And since you never made the reciprocal deposits into their hearts, since you never sought to help them fulfill their dreams and their desires, since you never asked what made their clocks tick or what filled their love tanks, you could never achieve truly authentic connection with the people around you. That is what drove you to this affair, which actually opened you up to us and to this intervention. But now, my friend, you are free. Free from the yoke that drove you to the sky politically—and into the ground relationally."

Jim sat on the ground with his legs crossed and with a coolness in his heart that he had not felt since his early college days. He suddenly remembered sitting on the quad in college with the grass underneath him and looking up at the sky, laughing with all of his might—the same belly laugh that had just rolled over his body like a freight train. He had not even noticed that it was missing all this time.

"I feel it," Jim replied calmly, wiping the last of the tears from his eyes with his fingertips. "I have been asleep for so long."

"Yes, you have. Yet the important thing is not how long you were asleep, but that you are awake now. Do not let regret or shame from the past steal the freedom you have found in this moment. You must look forward, not behind, for you have a great work ahead of you."

"Ah, and what might that be?" Jim chuckled cynically as he spoke. "I'm about to be a political hack once this affair hits the press. Maybe it's for the best after all. I was never much of a legislator anyway, always looking out for numero uno. What did I care about all those people? It was all a real shame."

"No, Jim. You are looking backwards already. You have a future ahead of you still, in politics. Three months from now a door is going to open for you, a shift onto the national scene. I need you to take it. You will feel unqualified initially, but what qualifies you now is not your knowledge or your experience, but your heart. Allow your heart to lead, and all of the necessary doors will be opened before you."

Jim could not completely fight back the smile that attempted to come over his face, so it showed up like a sly grin, like the bashful look you might see on a schoolboy when the girl he has a crush on walks into the room. Jim experienced great relief knowing that his days in politics had not come to a close, again not for selfish reasons, but deep down he had always known, ever since his early teenage years, that he was born to be a legislator. He had taken this calling down the wrong path, but it had a pure root that Jim felt ready in this moment to nurture again from the ground up if he had to.

"And now, I must leave you," Tatanka spoke sternly. The intensity of his gaze seemed to increase with each passing moment and never wane, like he was always angling toward a crescendo that only built and built.

"But what about the rest of the story, the history? And the vision I saw, of the compass rose encircling the earth? I know there is more, so much more. We just left off at the Philippines and Hawaii. I mean, we hardly broke into the 20th century, much less the 21st. I need to know more, I need to know—"

Tatanka interrupted him flatly. "Jim, there isn't time. You must go home. Your family needs you."

"But this place is outside of time," Jim rebutted. "How can you say there is no time? That doesn't make any sense."

"I exist in a world which is outside of your chronological time," Tatanka explained with a deep resounding patience in his voice. "But there is a different type of time, the moments that impact you forever, the markers in your life that shape who you are—the birth of a child, a graduation, a terminal diagnosis, a life-changing accident or simply a conversation that alters the way you see the world. These are the time markers that the Great Spirit both observes and orchestrates.

"You have already been struck" Tatanka went on, "with one of these moments, with your daughter this morning, which led to the freedom you found here. You do not have the emotional energy to process any more than you already have at this time. In fact, it is going to take you several years to fully unravel all that has been planted in your heart in these last few days. But do not grow discouraged or become disillusioned. This is a lifelong process. I will return to you on the eve of your next appointment. You will have more capacity then. There is still much to uncover."

"Well, at least give me a hint—*something*," Jim said with a touch of desperation in his voice. For days, he had been harboring on and off the hope that these encounters would just go away and cease for good, yet now he could feel a faint sense of fear to be back on his own again.

"Jim, you know more than you give yourself credit for. The specific episodes in history that people are constantly dwelling on will not do you any good unless you recognize the patterns that lie beneath them all. Without knowing the why behind the what, the motivating factor which drives the narrative, you will always be pouring over the past and never understanding the present or anticipating the future. Just think about the common threads of the eras that we covered."

"Well," Jim began slowly but somewhat assuredly, "I could see the ships from Europe coming to the new world, the trade routes that is, and all of the commodities invested like little seeds being planted on American soil, some of those being human slaves. Then I could see the ships going north and south, along the coast and inland, with the raw materials going north and the finished goods flowing south. Then I saw the wagon trails and the train tracks headed out West, with the raw materials coming back East and the manufactured products shipping out West, and then the coal ships carrying on where the tracks left off, launching out into the great blue to Hawaii and all the way across to Asia and down into the Caribbean. But that was as far as I could see."

"And those same routes," Tatanka picked up without missing a beat, "charging south right through Latin America to the great canal in Panama and eventually all the way down to Cape Horn and then east again, right back across the Atlantic. What does it all have it in common, Jim? Why can nothing, man or beast, stand in its way? And why does violence always surround it?"

Jim stopped for a moment to think. He had not realized it until this very second, but his brain pulsed and reeled from fatigue and he knew his cognition had nearly reached capacity. Yet he pressed through and tried to synthesize all of the puzzle pieces into one big picture.

"Let's see. The trade routes represent capital. You can't have explorers without financial backers. Columbus thought he would fund his expeditions with gold, but he found no gold. Instead, he took slaves to foot the bill. Financial backers always want a return on their investment."

Jim paused for a moment. "That's it! Return on investment. Ships cost a lot of money. So do colonies and slaves and horses and plows and seeds and factories and wagons and railroads and coal ships. And automobiles and airplanes and ocean liners, and all of the cargo they carry. They are all one man's work and another man's investment. The hired hand cares to a degree and will go a certain length to protect his livelihood. But the owner will do whatever it takes to protect his investment and to reap the return from it. That's why they always bring along their guns. It's not self protection—it's property protection.

"Guns protected the trade routes," Jim continued, "they drove the Indians back, they kept the slaves in their place, they kept the Union together, they held the Negroes down, they kept the tracks clear from buffaloes and from Redskins, they gained us

Hawaii and the Philippines and the Canal, and I suppose all the way to the ends of the earth—what I saw in the vision. But it's not about the guns at all. They are only the means to ensure that the investment is not lost, to guarantee a good rate of return."

"But Jim," Tatanka broke in again with deep patience in his voice. "Is it just the guns, the bombs, the tanks—the weapons themselves? Or is there more? Think about how they are used. What happened when a slave rebelled or tried to escape?"

"Well, when a runaway slave got caught, they made an example out of him. Or if they thought a slave might be plotting a rebellion, they made an example out of him and everyone around him. His family and friends—anybody who might be remotely involved."

"Yes, Jim. And did they just kill them or was there more?"

"Oh, they tortured those slaves mercilessly. Anybody who ran away or rebelled or posed a threat of any kind, sometimes just for looking at you the wrong way. They whipped them, beat them, branded them, burned them, hung them, mutilated them—and then lots of times they still killed them. They raped the females and humiliated the males. They split up families and whole communities."

"Why, Jim?" Tatanka probed. "Why not just shoot them, if it's all about the guns?"

Suddenly, a light bulb went off in Jim's head like an explosion of clarity as isolated incidents from world history all came into view in a single moment of time.

"Oh, no!" Jim nearly screamed with a mixture of amazement and horror. "Oh no, oh no! How did I not see this before?

It wasn't just the guns that kept them in place. It was fear—no, *terror*. They tortured the few to *terrorize* the masses. They wanted to make an example out of them in order to keep everybody else in their place, to keep them all working hard, to keep them all in line, to make sure they didn't even think about rising up or running away. It was the same with the raids and the massacres of the Native Americans, the reservations and the forced removals, the Trail of Tears. And the black codes and Jim Crow laws, the lynchings and the bombings and the KKK. Then the war on drugs, SWAT teams and mass incarceration, mandatory minimums and three strikes laws, the electric chair and solitary, millions of men and women locked behind bars.

"Oh no, oh no! And in Central and South America, the banana republics and the dictators, the School of the Americas and the coups, dirty wars and death squads, kidnappings, political imprisonment, torture, execution, mass graves—tens of thousands of disappearances and murders in El Salvador, Guatemala, Argentina, Chile—all for fruit and coffee and tea and mining and oil, all to terrorize the labor leaders and the nationalists fighting for living wages, fighting for the poor, fighting to keep their own resources for their own people. And what's worse, the silent millions who will never rise, who are destined to live their lives in the squalor of state endorsed poverty because they know all too well what happens to anyone who stands up to US hegemony.

"And the Middle East, oh no, the Middle East. Of course they hate us and chant, 'Death to America!' We've overthrown their democratically elected leaders, installed puppet governments, invaded their nations, trampled on their sacred sites, tortured prisoners beyond human limits and all for what—oil? Our infrastructure and pipelines benefit the richest of the rich, and what about the rest? What happens if they rise up and call for their fair share? Just more repression and fear.

"And Asia, oh no, oh no, the nukes. Hiroshima and Nagasaki. Whole cities wiped out in a single moment. Entire families, genealogies, gone from the face of the earth. And the radiation, the horrible slow deaths of those who weren't completely obliterated. Tens of thousands dead in an instant with the death toll rising by the hour. The vast majority, normal civilians—men, women and oh, the children—gone. From two bombs. And we have thousands of them, armed and ready, exponentially more powerful than those two. Aimed where? At the whole world? Anyone who crosses us the wrong way? If that's not terror—"

"Every empire in the history of the world has been built on terror, Jim," Tatanka broke in swiftly. "That is the answer. It's why the Romans crucified their enemies, sometimes right along the side of the road, to send a loud and clear signal to the whole world that you don't mess with Rome. Terror is the invisible hand which rules 24 hours a day, not just controlling people's actions, but their minds as well."

"Wait a second," Jim interrupted. "I see it, but—but I have never felt fear or terror like that in my entire life. What am I missing here?"

"The problem is," Tatanka continued, "the system works so well for some that they never even see it. But your black colleagues who grew up in Jim Crew certainly know about terror. They were taught as small children to jump through every hoop, to step off the sidewalk, to tip their hats, to sit in the back of the bus, to be on their toes every minute of every day or else their lives and the lives of their entire families were at risk. Roman citizens had all the rights in the world, but the people they conquered—watch out. It's the way every aspect of the natural world works. Everything operates according to the Law of the Strong."

"But America is such a peaceful place, and a prosperous place—"

"The male lion may look peaceful, calmly patrolling his territory, casually watching over his pride, but you can be sure that none of it was gained without a fight. At some point, he won the land by proving his strength, and he will either keep it or lose it by those same means. Just because a nation appears to be at peace does not mean it is tame or that it has no blood on its hands. It may just mean that it has proved its strength in the past and that it is only waiting to do so again, whenever that time comes."

"Wait," Jim interjected, "it seems like we are constantly at war abroad, constantly having to prove our strength."

"Yes and no," Tatanka began again. "The United States is officially at war with seven other nations at the moment. But your invisible hand permeates nearly every nation in the entire world. Your government has more than 800 military bases in 80 countries. That is territory gained one show of strength at a time. Now it is simply being maintained. There are more ways to frighten your enemies than to crucify people by the side of the road. Hit the insurrectionists hard and make an example of them, one way or another. The rest will fall into line. It's the way of empire, Jim. There is nothing new under the sun.

"Not too many world leaders," the enormous buffalo went on, "want to sign a death wish of crossing the United States of America. Just look at Saddam Hussein. Started on the CIA payroll as an assassin during an attempted regime change in 1958, he gained power five years later in another CIA-backed coup and partnered with US intelligence to hunt down and systematically murder thousands of his political enemies. He remained a strong ally for decades and was supported by your military even with full knowledge of his brutal chemical warfare against both soldiers and civilians during the Iran-Iraq War— that is, until he invaded oil and investment rich Kuwait in 1990 without your permission.

"His political repression and human rights abuses did not preclude him from being a strong ally as long as he remained in alignment with US economic interests. But once he crossed that line, it was the beginning of the end. After several failed assassination attempts in the 90s and a botched coup against his regime in 1996, there were no other options left but to invade. Then 19 men attacked your nation hailing from Saudi Arabia, UAE, Lebanon and Egypt, and your government decided to declare war against—Iraq?

"Every single one of your decision makers knew that Iraq had nothing to do with 9/11 and that there were no weapons of mass destruction, but that didn't matter to your government and it didn't matter to your media. They all lied through their teeth, determined to use 9/11 as a smokescreen to oust Saddam. First, the media villainized him with selective amnesia about his chemical warfare, which your government not only knew about but actually helped him to develop, allowing him to purchase deadly biological viruses such as anthrax and bubonic plague from an American supplier. Then when they finally got their man nine months after the invasion began, they plastered up his scraggly mug-shot for the whole world to see. And in the end, what's the message to world leaders? 'Don't mess with the US. If you cross us, we will not relent until we bring you down.'"

"And what about the message to the people of the world?" Jim jumped in. "Since we invaded Iraq in 2003, there have been nearly 200,000 documented civilian deaths from direct violence of the war, not counting combatants. Estimates of the total death toll from all aspects of the war top one million Iraqi civilians dead, with millions more displaced as refugees. I mean, we have dropped over 100,000 bombs on a nation about the size of California. How does that bring any sort of justice to the 3,000 Americans who died on 9/11? It just seems like death on top of more death."

"Jim," Tatanka echoed gravely, "the horrific attack against your nation on September 11th, 2001 was a great tragedy, but it was undeniably blowback—retaliation from Desert Storm a decade prior when your nation occupied the two most sacred sites in Islam, Mecca and Medina. Bin Laden was a Cold War ally who grew embittered by the half a million troops who flooded his nation and trampled on his religious laws and way of life. So instead of killing Russian infidels in Afghanistan as he was recruited to do, he started killing Americans.

"But Jim, think forward for a moment. Do you honestly believe there won't be any blowback from your invasion of Iraq, or that it hasn't already begun? What embittered Iraqi kid is going to be the next Osama bin Laden 10 or 20 years from now? And what is your nation going to do in response? What makes you think that this vicious cycle will ever end? Until the endless arms race and chain reaction of violence is broken, it will continue to be, as you said, death upon more death."

"Isn't it ironic," Jim reflected after a brief pause, "that we have declared war on terror, on the very idea of terror itself, when terror is built into our very DNA as a nation? We meddled on Middle East turf for 50 years and called it democracy. Then they struck back on our turf, and we called it terrorism?"

"It's the pirate and the emperor, Jim. The world has no grace for desperate people. Men who sell drugs in the inner city because there is no other economy. Women who sell their bodies for sex to feed their children. Men who pick up a gun or strap on a bomb to fight back against the powers to be. To the British Empire, the American revolutionaries were full blown terrorists. Remember the Tea Party, the Sons of Liberty? The only difference is that, against all odds, they won. So now, instead of going down in history as dead and forgotten insurrectionists, they are called patriots and founding fathers."

Jim sat for a moment in silence. He had no more questions to ask, just a heaviness which weighed over his entire being.

"The world has no grace for pirates," Tatanka continued,

"and they are too afraid to speak out against the emperor. So they settle into the status quo, and for most people, that's good enough. The American system works very well for its power brokers. So everyone just hums along and looks the other way, condemning those who live in poverty but refusing to look at the systems that marginalize them in the first place. Jim, we do not have time to cover any more ground. You must return to your family. But one last thing before you go. Do you see that hat?"

Tatanka lowered his head slightly, motioning toward the tile floor in front of Jim where his bright red cap had been lying ever since he had collapsed to the ground earlier. "Read me what it says, please."

"It says," Jim began as he slowly reached for the hat, "Make America Great Again."

"Put it back on your head," Tatanka said. "From now on, this is your new mandate—with one modification. The time is now to make America great, but not again, not as you have measured greatness in the past. Since the dawn of time, the world has operated according to the Law of the Strong. Every world power in history. Power corrupts. And absolute power corrupts absolutely.

"But, Jim, there is another way. There is a greater law, one that trumps the Law of the Strong every time—the Law of Love. This is your destiny, Jim, to live and to breathe and to legislate according to the Law of Love. To make America great, not again, but for the very first time."

"How, I mean, what exactly is the law of love?" Jim asked

as he rose to his feet, swooping up the cap with his hand and straightening it over his forehead.

"I'm so glad you asked," Tatanka replied with a sparkle in his cavernous eyes. "The Law of Love always prioritizes people over things. Whoever the Great Spirit puts in your path today, whether it be the Queen of England or a poor beggar on the side of the road—or your own wife—that person, according to the Law of Love, is the most important person in your world at that moment. Love gives you the grace to put the needs of others before your own, without the snare of selfish motivation. This is the Law of Love, the very heartbeat of the Great Spirit."

"But our nation's history," Jim responded, "is chock full of people who have fought with the Law of Love in their hearts—those who sought peace with the Native Americans, who risked their lives teaching slaves to read and helping them to escape through the Underground Railroad, the abolitionists and the civil rights workers, the war protestors and the investigative journalists who put their lives on the line to uncover injustice and oppression, the teachers and stay-at-home mothers, normal everyday working folks trying to make the world a better place—the list goes on and on."

"The history of your nation is not all bad as some make it out to be," Tatanka continued, "nor is it all good as others assert. There are those who have fought for love, yes, great numbers who have stood up to the powers that be and who have taken care of the vulnerable and the poor and the marginalized—but sadly, their voice has been drowned out time and time again. Peace treaties gave way to the Indian Removal

Act, Reconstruction collapsed into Jim Crow, the Civil Rights Movement triggered White Flight and the War on Drugs, globalism opened the door for imperialism, and immigration, oh, immigration—you're all a bunch of immigrants, you know. I hate to tell you that, Jim. Time and time and time again, the dominant voice which has continually steered the course of your nation has reverted back to one of military force and economic dominance—the Law of the Strong.

"You must always celebrate those who live with love in their hearts, the freedom fighters, and the victories they have achieved. But you can't stop there. You must join them, Jim. The people of your nation have no idea how many enemies you have around the globe because you keep the whole world under your thumb. But you allow one of those budding powers to rise up successfully and you will see—it will be the same old story, just the same old human story. People are the same everywhere you go. Now is the time for the voice of love, the heartbeat of the Great Spirit, to be the dominant voice in your nation to shape your future and the future of the world."

Suddenly, Jim remembered the words of the carabao just before he vanished, about seeing the Great Spirit face to face. "What about my meeting with the Great Spirit?" Jim blurted out. "Please, I would like to see him before you go."

"Jim, you have seen him. You have seen him in me. You have seen him in all of us." Tatanka paused and looked grave, but Jim did not relent. Finally after some time, he continued. "This is a hard thing you ask, but if you insist—"

Tatanka's voice trailed off, and a deep silence engulfed the room. The void Jim had felt prior to each of his encounters came over him once again, like the entire atmosphere had been siphoned out of the room in a single moment of time, but with a heightened level of intensity that he knew could never be put into words. Then with no warning, Jim's whole world exploded into a flash of light, and everything went perfectly white. Yet rather than the pain one would normally feel looking directly into the sun or some other intense light source, Jim experienced nothing but perfect peace and comfort all around him.

A soothing warmth radiated through his entire being, which made his body feel lighter than air, as if he might float away at any moment. He felt no shame, no sadness, no condemnation—only perfect acceptance and unconditional approval. The strength and impenetrable security of a father's embrace surrounded him as the softness and gentleness of a mother's kiss graced the moment. And somehow he knew—he did not know how he knew, but only that it came from a deep place in the core of his heart—that everything was going to be alright, that all of the problems and all of the conflict and all of the things that weighed so heavy on his mind every single day, that it was all going to work out and that he didn't have to worry anymore.

Jim did not want to move or even flinch for fear that the feeling might disappear and he might find himself back in the real world, which at this moment seemed immeasurably cold and dark by comparison to what he was currently experiencing. He was not quite sure if he could move even if he tried, his body feeling as comfortable as it did, but at the same time, he had an innate sense that he could move better and swifter than he ever had before in his entire life, even in his youthful days.

Just as this thought was milling around in his head, he heard a soothing voice which seemed to emanate out from the very center of the light. The stunning brightness that surrounded him was not flat or formless, but rather it had texture and weight and more dimensions than Jim could possibly describe, like the expanse of stars blanketing the night sky when you are deep in the country with no lights for miles and miles around.

The voice had no sharpness to it, no edges, and it exuded comfort like the sound of a light rain against a tin roof. The tones moved up and down with subtle inflection, but the rise and fall was completely predictable like the crashing of waves on the seashore or the crackling of a fire, which had a calming effect on Jim's soul. The words all carried a certain weight as if they were hand selected, each one resonating down to the very core of his being, producing a deep sense of both conviction and longing, as if they were carrying him deeper and deeper down the rabbit hole into Wonderland.

"Jim," the voice began, "I love you, more than you will ever know. You have not known me, not in a long time, but I have known you. I have watched you and carefully observed you. I have seen you grow, grow up to be a man, and I am proud of you. You knew me as a child, and you used to talk with me and sing songs to me. You used to laugh with me and run with me and pick flowers with me. But then you forgot, and you became callous and your heart grew hardened toward me. Eventually, you forgot that you ever knew me, and you moved on with your life.

"But I have seen you, not to punish you or to hurt you, but only to help you and to celebrate you. I care so much for you that you cannot fully comprehend, like the love you feel for your children, just magnified infinitely greater and stronger and wilder. I have seen your struggles, and I have seen your pain—your sad and lonely heart. This is why I have come. Not to upset or to disrupt you, although I knew this would be a necessary part of the process, but to heal you and to set you free. My intentions toward you are pure, and I am not motivated by anything other than a burning desire to see you live the best and fullest life possible.

"You have made many mistakes, Jim, grave errors which have hurt a lot of people—the people who are the very closest to you in this world. They know about the affair, Jim, I have shown it to them, and they were not surprised. Hurt, yes, but not surprised. They have seen your distance, felt your distance, like an aching void in each of their lives. It will take a long time for them to heal—the wounds you have inflicted are very deep.

"But you have turned your heart back to them—this was not my doing—you had to make that decision for yourself. And now that you have, I am granting you a clean slate and a new beginning. You do not deserve a second chance, but this is not about what you deserve. This is about my unending love for you. I have allowed you to feel my love, to see my love, to hear my love. When I leave, this feeling will leave with me. But remember that I am always with you and be sure to treasure this moment in your heart.

"Now I must go, Jim, never forget the love I have in my

heart for you. Never forget the love you have encountered in this place. Go and share it, Jim. With all the world. With your wife and your children. With your friends and neighbors. Even with your enemies and those you hate, or used to hate. There is no room for hate in a heart filled with love. This is your new job, Jim. To love. Love the people I put in your path each day and leave the rest up to me. I will visit you again, when your heart has had time to heal, when your family has had time to heal. Until then, never forget, Jim, never forget—my love."

And with that, the light and the warmth and the pitter-patter of the Great Spirit's voice were all gone, and Jim found himself in the pulsing heart of the busy terminal, its lifeblood beating and flowing all around him like the cacophonous chaos that had long ago become the constant backdrop of his life. Only now, after his encounter with the Great Spirit, did the noise and the frantic pace of it all stand out so starkly and so bluntly. The Great Spirit had left as gently as it had arrived, but Jim had not been prepared for the crash back into the throbbing pulse and pounding busyness of the airport and the world.

His head spun as he regained his bearings, and before he had time to even think about what had just occurred, he heard a voice call out, "Next!" He looked around only to discover that he was standing at the very front of the line. He walked across the hard tile floor to the counter and booked a direct flight home departing in less than two hours.

As he walked away from the counter, ticket in hand, he turned and tipped his cap to the woman at the desk who had helped him.

"Have a great day, ma'am, and thank you," he called out over his shoulder. Jim could not remember the last time he had interacted with someone in such a genuine and heartfelt way. Yet somehow he had felt an authentic connection with her as a person, as a fellow human being, even after such a short transaction.

That was strange, Jim thought as he headed toward security, falling in line with all of the other travelers pacing to and fro like ants moving along their invisible trajectories. Just then, he felt a nudge in his heart, not an audible voice but the faint echo of a whisper that said, *Get used to strange, Jim. It's your new normal.*

Jim stopped dead in his tracks as he felt the words penetrate his soul—just as the voice of the Great Spirit had several minutes before. Cold chills crept over the back of his neck as the hair on his arms stood on end. He shook his head slightly to see if he could dislodge the tingling down his spine, and he closed his eyes for just a few seconds as he drew in a deep breath. He removed the ball cap from his head and lowered it down into his line of sight—*Make America Great Again.*

Greatness, here I come, Jim thought as he placed the hat back on his head, looking out over the terminal full of people and finding a newfound love welling up in his heart for each and every one of them—for humanity itself.

Greatness, here I come.

BOOK II

XIV

The room spun as the light reflected and refracted off the sea of chandeliers which appeared to be swaying in sync with the pulsing crowd waltzing just beneath them. The scene reminded Jim of something out of *Beauty and the Beast*, a movie he had watched countless times when his daughter was young and when she ached with all of her heart to be a princess—the elegance and the grandeur and the rhythmic throbbing of the crowd dressed to the nines moving and whirling in perfect harmony as if an invisible puppeteer were pulling and drawing all of the strings simultaneously with faultless cadence.

Jim gripped his wife fiercely with his right arm, supporting her around her waist, while gently extending his left, providing a platform for her right hand as he led her this way and that around the ballroom—left foot, right foot, box step, forward, promenade. They moved as one unit, two parts of a whole, perfectly in step with one another as they had for years and years at events like this one.

Even when nothing but ice water ran through their veins for one other, they had learned to project grace and resilience on the dance floor and off. His career depended on it, and they both knew it all too well. Donor money does not discriminate and has a way of growing wings and flying away when facades start to crack and crumble. Which is precisely what began to happen when the first story detailing Jim's extramarital affair dropped like a bomb shell in the international press three months prior.

He anticipated that it would be painful and braced for the worst, but there is nothing in this world which could have prepared him for the whirlwind that hit him head on like a drunken melee pinning him in on all sides. He had come clean voluntarily, calling a press conference at the State House the week after his return home. His chief of staff thought he had lost his mind and begged him to keep it all under wraps.

"For the sake of your wife and kids, Jim," he bellowed. "For the sake of the whole entire state!"

But Jim knew he couldn't carry the weight of a secret like this one any longer, and he could already feel its crushing heft bearing down on him every minute of every day. He would rather die than be fated to live under the mind-numbing conviction that shouted him down in his thoughts during the day and in his dreams at night. He had let his family and his constituents and his home state of Georgia down, and now there was nothing left to do but to own up to his actions and to face the music like a man.

At first, the stories ran nonstop day and night. It seemed like every five minutes another news outlet jumped on the bandwagon, scathing Jim with the exact same details which he himself had disclosed openly, only in slightly different order. *In court, you get a break for pleading guilty,* Jim told himself as the phones in his office rang off the hook day after day after day. *But out here, in the real world, you get nothing—nothing but a full-on blitzkrieg.*

Jim knew he couldn't complain, that he deserved every jab, every cross and every uppercut thrown his way. But what hurt him the most were his faithful supporters who had been with him for years and even decades—the irate calls and messages and emails. His personal voicemail filled up within a half an hour of the initial press conference and stayed full no matter how hard he tried to clear out the torrent of fever-pitched word daggers.

Incense and outrage clouded the airwaves all around his life, and there was nothing Jim could do but apologetically mourn the loss—the loss of trust and relationship, family really, that he had built with decades of blood, sweat and tears. Now it felt as if everything was being torn apart at the seams and in places far more painful than the seams, places that didn't naturally divide in two.

He knew his family had it the worst, primarily since they had done nothing remotely wrong and because they weren't able to see it all coming. Although they were not complicit in any way, they still faced the same crippling onslaught bombarding them day and night. The only grace came in the way that one's mind goes totally numb after about 24 hours of incessant barraging and beyond that reverts to a sort of comatose state where the information is still accessible but the wires that patch through to the part of the brain which regulates emotional response have been completely severed.

The strangest phenomenon Jim witnessed, even in the raging

eye of the storm, was the apparent normalcy of his home, how on the surface everyone looked and acted as if nothing had happened, like normal human beings under completely normal circumstances. Yet it didn't take him long to realize that the façade was only an inch deep and that any errant word or action on his part could set the whole house off like a chain reaction. His wife's stroke had been relatively minor, and she was discharged only two days after being admitted with occasional bouts of dizziness but no paralysis to her face or limbs. Doctor's orders were to get plenty of rest, so she had already hunkered down in the house when the news of the affair first exploded across the media outlets.

Jim found his wife impossible to read under normal circumstances, so in the aftermath of a cataclysmic implosion like this one, he didn't even try. Silence ruled between them even more fiercely than before, and as with the phone calls and the news stories which rolled in one after the other, he faced it stoically. He was already used to being stonewalled by her, the difference now being that he recognized his lion's share of the guilt and found himself lingering around his wife like a guilty puppy who had just torn up a favorite pair of shoes or tracked muddy paw prints on a brand new couch. He would hover with his proverbial tail between his legs, too wise to make a peep but secretly hoping that she would open the door for conversation with a word or even an inviting look so that he could gush forth yet another round of apologies, exposing some new facet of his remorse which he had not up to this point been able to air.

Yet in the midst of it all, Jim kept reminding himself that it could have been a thousand times worse. His wife had not left him or kicked him out of the house. Instead, he had graciously been allowed to move into one of the guest bedrooms, where he welcomed the time alone for personal reflection and much-needed contemplation. Jim had not been the same man since his encounter with the Great Spirit, and not a moment passed that he did not think about the spirit animals who had appeared to him during his fateful trip to Barranco.

He had come away with a new mindfulness of others, the people surrounding him on a daily basis, and although she hated to admit it, his wife could not help but notice that a marked and substantial change had occurred in him. For starters, he wasn't as brazen and brash with his words as he used to be, and he appeared to be making a concerted effort to restrain his anger and bridle his tongue. She noticed it especially in the way he addressed their children. He was softer and more patient, traits she had not witnessed toward them since they were preschool age. Undoubtedly, this impacted her more than anything else.

Then there were the flowers and the spontaneous gifts. At first, she was annoyed when fresh cut tulips started showing up on the breakfast room table after a 15 year lull, and she shooed him away like a schoolboy when he approached her with little sirsees of dark chocolate or a piece of her favorite tiramisu from the bakery around the corner. She knew he was just buttering her up and watched and waited for the trickle of generosity to dry up like a seasonal stream in the blistering heat of summer. But if anything, the flow only picked up with time, and the small, succinct notes attached to each love offering began to chisel away at her heart, hardened by time and neglect toward her husband.

The notes weren't elaborate or even aesthetically appealing. He wrote on scraps of paper and sticky notes from the utility drawer like a typical clueless male, but the words carried a sense of rawness, an authenticity that struck her like the closing scene of a tragedy where the hero is unable to escape the cruel hand of fate and bows to his demise with nobility and resolve. She showed no signs of alleviating her blockade of any and all affection toward him, nor did she have any inclination to do so. Yet after three months of steady, persistent effort on his part, she was beginning to wonder what on earth had gotten into Jim Hamilton.

As they swirled around the room, their eyes darted to and fro scanning the faces of the other governors and their wives from all over the country who had gathered for the annual National Governors Association winter meeting, held this year in Washington, DC. They looked up at the massive 15-foot curtains and down at their feet and around the room at the ornate Chinese silk wall hangings and back down to the floor again to ensure that their steps remained in perfect sync.

She tried with all of her might not to look at his face, which she always attempted to avoid while dancing—not that she had ever caught him looking back. But occasionally this night, his eyes caught hers and the little inkling of a smile that came over his checks and the twinkle along the round edges of his irises spoke into her soul something that a hundred flower arrangements or a thousand apologies could never have communicated. She saw the old Jim, the man she had married 22 years ago. And it scared her to death.

XV

The next morning, Jim awoke to the clamoring of his hotel phone, which rattled the glass top of the side table adjacent to his bed like the roar of rumble strips on the side of the highway when you drift off at the wheel. He looked at it strangely as if it were something out of a classic movie from his childhood and picked up the receiver as the retractable cord dutifully uncoiled.

"Hello," Jim spoke hesitantly into the handset.

"Jim," the voice on the other end came through loud and clear. "Jim Hamilton?"

"Yes," Jim responded, fully expecting to be asked what he wanted for breakfast or whether or not he wanted turndown service.

"Jim, you old dog! This is Larry Wade. I heard you were in DC for the weekend."

"Larry?" Jim responded quizzically. "How did you get this number? And who on earth still uses hotel phones? I didn't even know these ancient things still worked. Why didn't you just call me on my cell?"

"I lost your number. Went to look it up today and—these twenty-something aids have been tinkering with my phone, updating it they say, but now I can't find a flippin' thing. Well, you know how it goes. Listen, Jim, I've got something for you. How soon can you meet me at the Jefferson, on 16th Street? Breakfast on me."

"I mean," Jim thought out loud, "our program starts at nine, and I've got committee at 10. This better be good, Larry."

"Oh, it's good, Jim. Very good. Meet me in 30? I'll be in the lobby."

Jim hesitated for a moment to see if his brain had the where-withal so early in the morning to manufacture a decent excuse, and seeing that nothing came to mind, he relented. "Alright, I'll be there," he breathed out in annoyed acquiescence and then paused again. "This better be good."

Jim hung up the receiver and sprang from the bed to hop into the shower. He had not seen Larry Wade since he had left the Georgia House of Representatives to take a job as a DC lobbyist more than five years prior. The two had always gotten along, and Jim thought highly of Larry for his professional integrity and for his legislative ingenuity. He wondered as he draped his pajamas over the back of a chair what Larry could possibly want to discuss with him so urgently.

As Jim sped across town in the back of a yellow cab, he looked out over the nation's capital as a sense of unfulfilled longing overtook him, mingled with a hint of bitter regret. Up until three months ago, his political career like his resume had been immaculate, and he had been told by party insiders that he could not have a better rap sheet for a presidential nomination somewhere down the road. Although he had not articulated this aspiration and hidden desire of his heart to anyone other than his very closest inner circle, political analysts and reporters would occasionally hint at the possibility of a Jim Hamilton presidential run. He had been dealt a killer hand and had always played his cards just right.

Yet as he crossed over the National Mall on 14th Street with the National Monument in full view and only blocks from the White House, Jim mourned the loss of his oldest and most revered dream. And for what? Because he couldn't control his most primitive desires and because his relational currency had dipped so low that he recklessly gambled his entire political career to fill the void. Jim hid his face with his hand as a slow trickle of tears inched down both cheeks. He pressed his forehead against the cold glass window and closed his eyes as he stomached the enormity of his gaffe for the thousandth time. The pain had abated somewhat as time marched along, but it never fully went away. *Why, Jim?* He kept asking himself. *Why?*

Before he knew it, he had arrived at the entrance of the prestigious Jefferson Hotel with its stately golden doors encased on either side by two large black pillars and covered by a large black and white awning overhead, giving it the semblance of a gaping lion's mouth or the modern version of a Roman entryway to the temple of some obscure god.

Jim found Larry in the lobby as promised, and after a few minutes of getting reacquainted, they sauntered over to The Greenhouse for breakfast under the magnificent arched skylight filtering in the morning sun over their heads.

"Jim, let me cut straight to the chase here," Larry began, leaning in over the small, square table as if he were afraid someone nearby might overhear. "You know all of the turmoil at the UN right now. It's a real mess. Glowkoski is the worst kind of pushover with no hint of a backbone and, Jim, we've got to get him out. This administration has been eyeing you for months, but then—well, you know—then you flew off the radar. But things have just gotten so much worse, and, what I'm telling you is that they are willing to let the water under the bridge go if you will resign and take the spot."

Jim's mind reeled. He cocked his head back and flattened out his shoulders as he processed all that Larry had just laid before him.

"You are telling me," Jim started slowly and intentionally, "that the President wants me to serve as the US Ambassador to the UN—after the affair, after everything. Are you off your rocker?"

"Jim, this is no joke. You have the pedigree for it, plus," Larry leaned in even closer, "you have guts. Nobody knows how to lead around here anymore. You've got what it takes and you know it. We all think you're the man for the job." Larry leaned back in his chair and lifted his arms up with hands outstretched as if to indicate that he had made his point.

"Who in the world is this 'we' you're talking about?" Jim shot back. "I thought you were a lobbyist for DTE Electric?"

"Don't you ever watch C-SPAN, Jim? I've been the President's body man for the past two years. He would have contacted you directly, but he knew you and I go way back. He wants to meet ASAP, before you leave for home if we can swing it. What do you say, Jim, old boy?"

"I mean," Jim tripped on his words a little as blood rushed to his cheeks and his face became flushed. "I mean, I just can't believe—of course, I mean, of course I'll meet with the President. I just don't, I'm just not promising anything. And no, I don't watch C-SPAN."

"That's a start, Jim. I will let him know right away. Give me your cell phone number again so I don't have to track you down on any more landlines."

Jim chuckled as he pulled out his phone to share his contact with Larry. Gripping the device, he could feel his hands trembling as the weight of the invitation began to sink in. He quickly pulled his hands below the table to avoid showing any visible signs of weakness, and he took a long, deep breath to regain his composure. *If I were alone*, he thought in light of all the crying he had been doing lately, *I'd be a total mess right now.*

Jim's head was still spinning as he catapulted out of the golden double doors of the Jefferson and turned left onto the sidewalk in front of the hotel. He intentionally did not call a cab right away to mull over the potential ramifications of such an abrupt and unexpected summons. Less than an hour prior, he had been mourning the death of his political aspirations, and now, suddenly and without any forewarning whatsoever, they were on the verge of being resurrected in a monumental way.

XVI

After several minutes of walking, Jim realized that he had been frantically pacing the long blocks of 16th Street, and he made a concerted effort to ease his gait, his breathing and his racing mind. He studied a row of three-story brick townhouses all sharing a narrow wrought iron fence, which was drowning in an explosion of pink carnations draping over and through the black bars and spires as if to declare that their beauty would not be held back by man-made constraints.

As he admired the tumbling and sprawling flowers, a strange yet familiar feeling came over him like a weight pressing down on him from overhead. He stopped mid-step and looked up to see what had come over him, and as he did, he heard a faint whisper from somewhere down below which would have been completely imperceptible at his former pace.

He instinctively shifted his gaze downward and caught sight of a small black and yellow bird with a white stripe running down the length of both wings. It immediately flew up and landed on a tulip poplar branch about eye level with Jim, and the vacuum of time and space that Jim had grown so accustomed to during his trip to Peru crashed over him in a single instant like a barreling tidal wave.

Jim knew that the visitation Tatanka had forewarned him of in the airport had finally arrived, and although he had anticipated this moment for months, the intensity and the weight of the sensation that encompassed him caught him off guard. He had forgotten the overwhelming feeling of hyper-awareness which accompanied these encounters, the unparalleled keenness of his senses and the resonating internal voice of conscience which reverberated through his core like the sound of dynamite ripping through an underground mine far below the earth.

"Jim," the little bird began in a high-pitched but powerful voice which had a certain melodic quality to it. "You know why I have come. Do you recognize me or know what I represent?"

Jim had to catch his breath as he swallowed hard and licked his parched lips before attempting to respond.

"I know you are sent by the Great Spirit," Jim replied, "but I don't recognize you, no. I don't believe I have ever seen a bird with quite your coloration before."

"Think hard, Jim. Just take a moment."

Jim closed his eyes in compliance, and suddenly an image of a rainforest filled his mind. He could see the vast canopy of bright green treetops stretching as far as the eye could see with a wide, gushing river cutting through the landscape, winding this way and that until its trail disappeared just below the horizon. The scene descended down through the thick mesh of enormous trees, zooming in further and further until he could see a research substation built along the banks of the Orinoco River where he had spent several weeks the summer before his junior year of college.

"Venezuela!" Jim exclaimed. "How could I forget? You, you're a troupial. You used to wake me up every morning at Dr. Canton's research station." Jim paused and wrinkled his nose. "I'll never forgive you for that, by the way."

"Very funny, Jim," the small bird responded. "What else do you remember?"

"Let's see. I remember that you are the national bird of Venezuela. And your song, I will never forget the cacophonous, I mean harmonious sound of trills ringing through the camp. Whatever you do, don't visit the Orinoco River Basin during troupial mating season. Oh, and the time one of your friends pooped on my hammock. I could never get that stain out no matter how hard I scrubbed."

"Quite the recollection, my friend," the troupial said with a subtle shake of its black and white wings. "I can assure you that I had nothing to do with it. My name is Bolívar, after Simón Bolívar, or as the people affectionately called him, El Libertador. Tell me, what do you know about him?"

"Wait just a minute," Jim said, pulling his hands out of his pockets and gesturing rather madly with upturned palms. "What about this offer Larry Wade just put on the table? I thought you were here to give me an answer, to help me out. What do I do? I mean, what I am going to say to the President when he asks me to be his UN ambassador of all things? I mean, what's my family going to say? They just went through the ringer and now—"

"Jim, slow down. I'm not a Magic Eight Ball. You are a grown man fully capable of making decisions all by yourself. Besides, think back to what Tatanka said."

Jim froze in contemplation for a moment before answering. "He said that a door would open in three months and that I would feel unqualified—but that I should take it."

"Ok, how long has it been?" Bolívar questioned.

"Three months exactly," Jim replied.

"And, do you feel disqualified?" Bolívar probed further.

"More than words can express," Jim said with a sigh.

"Perfect!" the bird chirped with another slight shake of its wings. "There, you have your answer. Now can we get on with it, please?"

"Wait just a minute," Jim rebutted tersely. "How can we jump right back into another history lesson with my mind spinning a million miles per second. I mean, this is going to change everything. This, I just, I have never even been to Asia or Africa or half of Europe. Or to the Middle East. I'm kind of a Georgia homebody."

"Listen, Jim. I know this is brand new information to you and probably quite a shock. But you have to understand that I have a specific purpose in appearing to you today that I must fulfill. It's my job, so to speak. I am limited to my assignment by the Great Spirit. I realize you are experiencing a lot of internal upheaval right now, and I sympathize with you—but I also realize that the Great Spirit knows what you need better than you know it yourself. So you must trust that by the end of our time together, you will have precisely what you need. Does that make sense?"

Jim took a deep breath, slipped his right hand back into his pants pocket and nodded in assent as he shifted his weight forward to the balls of his feet.

"Fabulous," the troupial continued. "Now, tell me. What do you know about Simón Bolívar?"

"Hmm, I know he fought for the secession of Venezuela, Colombia, Panama and a handful of other Latin American nations from Spanish rule, sometime after the turn of the 19th century."

"Was he successful?" Bolívar probed further.

"Well, yes and no. He ultimately prevailed against the Spanish Empire and united a bloc of South and Central American nations together with the hopes of creating a sort of United States in Latin America. But in the end, he couldn't hold it all together, and the countries each broke off and formed their own independent governments. He famously said on his deathbed, 'All who served the revolution have plowed the sea,' because he failed to unite the region following its secession from Spain."

"Very good. Now, where have you heard his name in more recent history?"

Jim paused to think. "Chávez. The Bolivarian Revolution. That guy was a real maniac. Didn't he get the memo from the USSR that the socialism experiment has failed once and for all?"

"I suppose not. Tell me, Jim. What do you know about Hugo Chávez concretely, factually that is?"

"Well, I know he was a socialist dictator who ran his country into the ground. He took a thriving oil economy and imploded it from the inside out. I mean, come on, there are bread lines in Venezuela right now. People are starving. It's a real mess."

"Jim, the GDP per capita in Venezuela rose from \$4,105 in 1999 to \$10,810 in 2011 under Chávez's leadership. Doesn't sound like much of an implosion to me. Plus, there were bread lines in the US during the Great Depression. What's the difference?"

"That was the 1930s," Jim said with a huff. "I'm talking

about almost a century later. We've come a long, long way since then in terms of development."

"And Venezuela, what about their development? Have they been allowed to develop in the same way as the United States? Are there any other factors at play in their history that might hinder them from, as you call it, development?"

"Well, of course. The Monroe Doctrine was issued just a few years after Bolívar led the region's secession from Spain. So essentially, they went from being under the thumb of one world power to another. The United States had their eyes on the canal, so after taking about half of Mexico in the mid-19th Century, they worked their way through Central America down to Panama pretty quick."

"Did they stop there?" Bolívar asked.

"Of course not. By the turn of the 20th Century, the US had a pretty good foothold on the region. And from there, we just spread our wings to basically every corner of Latin America."

"So would you say that American presence helped or impeded the growth of the Latin American economy?"

"Well, that depends. When presidents and national leaders were willing to play the game, then yes. US investment in Latin America skyrocketed during the 20th Century, and frankly our corporate presence ushered in a whole new era of prosperity in the entire hemisphere, coming off the back of dying European imperialism."

"Prosperity for who?" the little bird asked, shifting its gaze and looking Jim directly in the eyes. "The common people? What is the difference between what the US has done in Latin

America than say Spain or Portugal? Do you think Bolívar would be happy with the new terms as they stand today for his beloved region of the world?"

"Of course not. But he was an absolutist. He didn't want to be ruled by anyone. I guess nobody does. But the reality is, there are global players at work, and small developing nations like Venezuela are going to be dominated by somebody. Exploitation is the name of the game, and there is just no way around it, I'm afraid."

"Is that so? No way around it? Or did Chávez find a way?"

Jim looked off, breaking the intense gaze of the troupial. "I guess, in a sense, he found a different way. But look at the suffering he caused because of it. He made his point standing up to the United States, but at what cost?"

"Let's see, Jim. He rewrote the constitution to work for the poor and working people rather than the wealthy, redirecting the nation's oil revenue away from multinational corporations to social missions in his own country. In 1998, about 6 million children in Venezuela attended school. By 2011, that number more than doubled to 13 million. Roughly 1.5 million Venezuelans learned to read and write under the Mission Robinson literacy campaign to the extent that UNESCO declared in 2005 that Venezuela had eradicated illiteracy.

"He created new universities, "Bolívar went on, "resulting in the number of students who received collegiate and professional training to rise from 900,000 in 1998 to 2.3 million in 2011. Unemployment fell from 14.5% in 1999 to 7.8% in 2011. He provided free universal healthcare, causing the number of doctors to increase by 400%, the infant mortality rate to fall by 49% and the average life expectancy to increase by more than two years, all from 1998 to 2011. In 1999, the year Hugo Chávez was sworn in as president, the poverty rate in Venezuela stood at 42.8%. By 2011, it had fallen to 26.5%. Extreme poverty was reduced in those same years from 16.6% to 7%. Tell me, Jim, does that all sound so bad?"

"But he was a strongman—"

"Jim, like him or not, Hugo Chávez was the democratically elected president of a sovereign nation. He won all four of his presidential elections outright in an electoral system that former US President Jimmy Carter described as the best in the world. In his last full term as president, Chávez won 63% of the national vote."

"Then why did his own people try to overthrow him in 2002?"

"His own people rescued him in 2002. He was kidnapped and would have been assassinated if it weren't for the popular uprising of the Venezuelan public who protested in the streets of Caracas nearly one million strong and a loyal military which returned him to power just 48 hours later. The United States had a heavy hand, and a fat wallet, in instigating not only the coup, but opposition to Chávez for the rest of his career, pumping millions upon millions of dollars into opposition groups aimed at discrediting him and bringing him down—dead or alive."

"Why did the US government want him out of power so desperately," Jim reflected, "if what you are saying is true?"

"You already said it yourself, Jim. He took a stand against US hegemony in Latin America. He stood up to the ruling elite in his nation and their stateside counterparts who siphoned out every last penny of oil revenue from a resource-rich nation where the majority of its citizens had been kept dirt poor for 150 years. Before Chávez took power, the capital city of Caracas was more slum than city, inundated and surrounded by shantytowns—in the center of the world's fourth largest oil exporter.

"He refused to submit the people of his nation," Bolívar continued, "to the crippling debt infrastructure packages from the World Bank and the International Monetary Fund that the US State Department has pushed down the throats of every single Central and South American country. The story is the same everywhere you go. The central governments of these small nations are coerced by threat of military force into taking out hundreds of millions of dollars worth of loans, which they then give right back to US multinational corporations who are contracted to build infrastructure that only benefits the wealthy, ruling class—people who look a lot like you, Jim—then the rest of the population is left holding the debt. A few years later, when the nation can no longer service their debt, they are forced into a restructure deal, requiring them to privatize their industries and government services—everything from natural resource production and power plants to schools and prisons—and sell them off to global investors.

"Most national leaders who resist don't live to tell the tale—Omar Torrijos in Panama, Jaime Roldós in Ecuador, Jacobo

Árbenz in Guatemala, Salvador Allende in Chile, to name a few—but Chávez beat the odds, and he championed the people. He sent a loud and clear message that America's Backyard is full of real people with real lives and real communities and that they aren't going to accept the status quo of relentless exploitation by their overbearing military super power neighbor to the north.

"And perhaps worst of all, he inspired a whole slew of others to do the same. One voice can have more of an impact than you realize—a single voice sounding a note that no one else is singing and that therefore no one else is hearing. But once they hear it and it resonates in the depth of their souls, they can't forget it."

"So are you pitching him as some sort of revolutionary or something?" Jim probed.

"Exactamente. That's precisely what he was—and still is. He had some major flaws and was far from perfect. But his movement lives on, despite the fact that your press has absolutely zero coverage of it. Millions upon millions of destitute people pulled out of poverty. Entire communities educated and put to work with decent wages for the first time ever. New roads and bridges, universities and hospitals, improved infrastructure and housing. All that wealth which failed to trickle down for more than a century, suddenly flowing to the very least like a mighty torrent of hope."

"Well, if what you're saying is true," Jim said thoughtfully, "then why does every major news outlet adamantly disagree?"

The troupial narrowed its gaze. "Jim, do you know how

many corporations control the media that you read and watch every day?"

"I don't know, probably three dozen or so."

"No, Jim. There are six. And they control 90% of all news media in the US. Thirty years ago there were 50. But due to mergers and buyouts, there are about 200 media executives who control every word of news you watch, read and then repeat. And can you guess whose interests they are more aligned with—the working poor in Venezuela or the multinational corporations who desperately want to privatize Venezualan oil production?

"When your nation backed Juan Guaidó," the troupial continued, "in declaring himself the appointed interim president of Venezuela—without an election of course—guess what was the first thing he tried to do? Privatize the oil. Coup d'etats used to be secretive affairs, but apparently after a century of carrying them out privately, they have become more palatable to your people. And what did they do to discredit the sitting democratically elected president, Nicolás Maduro? They shouted from the mountain tops that the elections were rigged.

"Jim, if you say something enough, loud enough and long enough, it eventually becomes accepted as people's reality. The international observers sent to Venezuela to verify the 2018 presidential election described it as 'fraud-proof.' They said that from start to finish, every stage of the election process was monitored by representatives of both contending parties. They provided a unanimous report that the elections were 'conducted fairly' and that 'the election conditions were not biased.' Yet why did every single major news outlet in your nation still cry foul?"

"Listen, Chávez might have had his day," Jim responded with a hint of irritation in his voice, "but anybody with a shred of sense in their head knew it couldn't last. It's a total disaster down there right now. Hyperinflation over a million percent. Grocery stores are empty. More than four million refugees have fled the country. How's that for a nail in the coffin of your so-called revolutionary?"

"Did anything happen that you know of between the death of Hugo Chávez and today that could have caused such extreme economic conditions?"

"Yeah, it's called socialism." Jim could not hide his exasperation. "I don't know why you keep pressing this issue. Socialism always works for a while, then you hit a bump in the road and it all falls apart. Venezuela is an oil economy. The price of oil plummeted in 2014 and 2015, and they couldn't recover. It's not that complicated."

"Venezuela has the largest proven oil reserves in the world," Bolívar replied evenly, "an estimated 300 billion barrels. When oil prices fall, under normal circumstances, you borrow against the reserves and keep on trucking. Has anything else significant happened?

"I don't know. You're obviously angling at something here."

"Yes, Jim," the troupial answered, ruffling its feathers and then settling back down onto its branch. "In 2015, the Obama administration declared Venezuela a threat to US national security—although the record is clear that it would be much more accurate the other way around—and began imposing sanctions. In 2017, under the current administration, these sanctions were ratcheted up to levels that Latin America hasn't seen since the US economic strangulation of the Sandinista government in Nicaragua in the 1980s—a blow the Nicaraguan economy has never recovered from to this day. In 2016, the year after Obama's sanctions began in Venezuela, the inflation rate jumped to 800%. In 2018, following the most recent round of sanctions, inflation skyrocketed to 1,698,488%. Say what you will about socialism, hyperinflation like that could only be the result of severe economic warfare.

"In addition to the sanctions, the United States has waged an all-out banking war against Venezuela, forcing Citibank to close the bank account of the Central Bank of Venezuela in 2016 and creating a complete financial blockade of all transactions in and out of the nation. Venezuela's state oil company based in the US, Citgo, can't even transfer profits back to the government to provide assistance to its citizens who are in desperate need. An estimated 40,000 people died as a result of the sanctions from 2017 to 2018, and those numbers are only predicted to continue unless something happens. The United States is simultaneously trying to drive the economy into the ground while pushing for regime change. Do you remember the last time the United States crippled a nation with sanctions and pushed for a changing of the guard?"

"Are you referring to Iraq?" Jim asked quizzically.

"Bingo. Hundreds of thousands were left dead from the sanctions between 1991 and 2003, which led up to the invasion of

Iraq later that year. Jim, do you see any patterns developing here? What do these two nations have in common?"

Jim paused to think for a moment. "They are both major oil economies. And founding members of OPEC."

"Precisely. And do you remember a fateful visit which was described as a slap in the face to the United States just one year before 9/11?"

Jim drew a blank and prompted the troupial to go on.

"Immediately after being elected president," Bolívar continued, "Chávez toured all of the OPEC nations and called for solidarity on long-ignored oil production quotas. When Chávez took office in February of 1999, oil prices had dipped to a 50-year low, selling for just $19.15 per barrel. By November of 2000, they had risen to nearly $50 per barrel. By rallying the OPEC nations, Chávez was able to drive international oil prices up by creating a united front among member nations to limit the total amount of oil produced, urging each country to stand firm on their quotas. Supply goes down, prices go up. Before this time, member nations would regularly cheat on their quotas and produce more than they were allotted, reaping a short term gain for themselves but leading to a lower price of oil for everyone—a practice Venezuela had been historically notorious for.

"When Chávez met with Saddam Hussein in August of 2000, it was seen as an affront to the United States because he was the first head of state to meet with Hussein in the decade since the Gulf War. The reorganization of OPEC represented a major threat, not only to the American way of life, but even more specifically to the US military, which is the single largest consumer of oil in the world, using more than 100 million barrels of oil per year. From that perspective, Venezuela and especially Chávez suddenly did pose a sort of existential threat to US global hegemony. Less than two years after that meeting, the United States backed a military coup against Chávez. Eleven months after the coup, the US military invaded Iraq with an army of over 175,000 soldiers.

"Chávez survived the coup," Bolívar went on, "and rising oil prices allowed him to invest a tremendous amount of money into his Bolivarian missions to serve the poor. Love him or hate him, Hugo Chávez brought an incredible amount of prosperity to the poorest of the poor all across his nation. Food, medicine, jobs, healthcare, housing—improving the everyday lives of an untold number of individuals, neighborhoods and communities. Just because someone lives in a slum or a shantytown doesn't mean they are any less human. Or because they are born in another nation with brown skin doesn't mean they deserve to be exploited. You can't measure a nation by its output or GDP or any other metric that the global investment elite like to use to justify meddling in everybody's business all over the globe. Life is measured by people, and when we miss that one point, we miss everything."

"So you're saying," Jim responded slowly and intentionally, "that we have painted guys like Chávez and Maduro as dictators and total monsters but that in reality they are heroes?"

"Well, I suppose it depends on who you ask" replied Bolívar. "Robin Hood was a hero to the poor, but I can't imagine the rich had much nice to say about him. And who do you think has more sway in the international news articles you read about global leaders—the rich or the poor? Jim, you will never have an answer to your question until you take the time to dig deeper and listen to the heartbeat of the people—Chávez's people— the poor Venezuelans who have absolutely no voice in your world. Are Chávez and Maduro saints? Of course not. They are politicians and military leaders. But the truth is, the majority of what you read about them has been intentionally and system- atically fabricated to fit a narrative with the sole purpose of justifying your nation's decision to illegally intervene.

"Just consider the dictator claim that is constantly thrown around by your media outlets. How can a democratically elected president with vast popular support and an independently veri- fied electoral system be a dictator? Yet the accusation itself has power, and due to its endless repetition, it has become reality in the minds of your entire generation, even though the claim is completely fabricated. Now, Chávez and Maduro are un- questionably socialist. But since when did being a socialist or a left-winger or a purple Martian from outer space give anyone the right to forcefully remove a civil servant in a sovereign nation from democratically elected office?

"The point that everyone in your media loves to argue is that socialism doesn't work. But it is entirely the wrong point. The question is not whether *socialism* works or not—but whether *democracy* is allowed to work in a world under US hegemony. In a true democracy, the people are free to choose any type of government they want. So if a Latin American nation that has been ravaged by centuries of European colonialism followed by a century of American imperialism and that has seen the absolute worst of the corrupt and oppressive underbelly of capitalism—if the majority of the people in that nation want to give socialism a try, then they ought to have the democratic right to do so.

"Yet the reality is that the United States government has violently cracked down on every single leftist and even remotely socialist regime to arise in Latin America over the past 100 years. And why? Because they pose the single greatest threat to US economic interests in the hemisphere, as well as the economic interests of your European allies. The United States inherited a very profitable colonial infrastructure in Latin America from your European predecessors, and your track record proves that you have no intention of letting go one inch.

"Don't be distracted by those who want to constantly pit socialism versus capitalism. This is about freedom and democracy. Your nation's century-long crusade in Latin America is not a war of ideology as your media has framed it, but a ruthless war to maintain economic dominance—not accompanied by the *promotion* of freedom and democracy, but rather at the very *expense* of it."

The troupial paused and Jim had no words, and for a long moment, silence reigned between them.

"Jim," Bolívar finally picked back up, "what your government is doing in Venezuela is criminal, and you have to face that fact. It may come with the turf of being the lone world superpower, but it doesn't mean that you're not violating the same international law you claim to uphold all over the world.

When wars, economic or otherwise, are fought for green—or for black sludge underneath the earth—that is called imperialism. And if that's what the United States of America wants to be all about, then so be it. But at least have the decency to call it for what it is. The rest of the world already knows. It's your people who seem to be the last on the planet to *wake up*."

With that, the little troupial flashed its wings and darted off like lightning into the morning air. Jim took a deep breath as the weight of the encounter lifted from his shoulders like a lead blanket after an X-ray. His body felt light but his heart carried a new heaviness which he had never before experienced. Jim lingered for a few moments studying the empty tree where the small bird had just been and then resumed his saunter down 16th Street.

He began to replay the conversation over again in his mind as he fought a strong sensation of insecurity rising up from deep in his gut. He felt like he might throw up, but he was afraid that if he stopped moving, it would grow worse. So he quickened his pace and stretched his neck up to the sky as if to beg for reprieve from the gray and white clouds which blanketed the heavens above him.

As he walked, he reached into his pocket for his cell phone and instructed Siri to dial his wife. As the phone rang, Jim thought there was no way he could sit through a whole day of Governor's Association meetings.

"Hi, Jim," the voice resounded flatly on the other end.

"Hi, hon," Jim replied, taking another long breath. "Are you busy?"

"What do you mean? Aren't you at the meeting? I thought you had a plenary session at nine."

"I do. I mean, I did. Something's come up. Can you meet me for breakfast? Where are you anyway?"

"I'm still at the hotel. But Jim, I told Michelle Ryan that I would meet her in half an hour at the National Gallery."

"Well, call her and cancel—this is big, babe. Real big."

"Babe! I hate it when you call me babe. Like I'm some kind of cheap side hustle. This is just like you, Jim, shirking your commitments and demanding that everybody drop what they're doing to suit your schedule. I haven't seen Michelle in years, plus she has some design prospects that really might pan out for me."

"Penny, you have to trust me. Listen, meet me in the lobby in 10 minutes. It won't take long, and then you can meet up with Michelle. *Please.*"

Jim's plea was met with silence on the other end of the line, which tortured him more than any words could have. After a long pause, his wife's voice came back on.

"Oh, alright," she acquiesced. "But you better not be late."

Before Jim could get in another word, the call ended. He slipped his phone back into his pocket and darted toward the street, waving his arm frantically to hail the first cab he saw.

XVII

Fifteen minutes later, Jim exploded out of the cab in front of the Mandarin Oriental Hotel, where he and his wife were staying for the weekend. He found her in the lobby staring rather crossly at him as he walked across the glimmering marble floor to the white suede armchair where she sat, legs crossed, tapping her left foot pointedly.

"You're late," she said calmly without shifting her gaze. "This better be good, Jim."

"Listen, Penny," Jim began as he slipped into a matching chair next to hers, "you know how we used to dream and aspire together about building a life here, in DC, on the national stage, and I know that we haven't talked like that in years but—"

"You're ranting, Jim," interrupted Penny. "What on earth are you babbling about? I really hope this is going somewhere."

"Yes, well, of course it's going somewhere. I'm just trying to give you some context before I tell you, because it's going to be a joint decision, I mean, you are just as much a part of this process as I am—"

"What decision? What process?" Penny questioned, looking annoyed. You're talking like a madman. Can you please just spit it out already?"

"The president," Jim said, wiping his brow with the back of his hand and leaning in slightly, "he has asked me to be his next Ambassador to the United Nations."

Stunned silence swept over Penny as her face grew wan and her features froze in a moment of pure puzzlement. After several moments, she broke the silence.

"How could he?!" she raved like an erupting volcano that had been mistaken for dormant. "Your career—your career is supposed to be over. It's what everyone has been saying for months. What, how could this be? Jim Hamilton, if you're putting me on—"

Jim stared at his wife wide-eyed, completely taken aback by her response. "I thought you would be happy, or at least a little excited. It's our dream—it's finally here."

"Are you totally clueless? You are such a typical male. Our dream? Our dream before you shacked up with some Hispanic hussy for all the world to see, running off and lying to all of us like that. I knew you had no regard for me and the kids long ago, I got that message, Jim. But your staff and your donors, the congress and what about the people? All the people of the state of Georgia who believed in you, who cast their vote for you—you, Jim, to represent them, to fight for them. All you know how to do is fight for yourself. You are something else. I don't know how to be excited for you anymore."

"It's not me, Penny," Jim finally spoke after a long moment of mournful silence. "This is us, our chance to reinvent ourselves, to write a new chapter together."

"There is no us anymore, Jim." Penny lowered her head into her hands just in time to hide the tears which began flowing like a torrential current at flood season. For a long time, Jim sat paralyzed unsure whether to reach out his hand and try to comfort his wife or to be still and wait out the storm. He ultimately decided on the latter and found himself silently praying—to whom he did not know. *Help us. Please help us,* he repeated over and over in an almost inaudible whisper.

Several minutes passed as wave after wave of violent sobs swept over his wife's body, causing her chest and back to heave up and down at sporadic intervals. Frozen by the fear of doing the wrong thing, Jim sat totally motionless for as long as he could. Finally, he rose from his seat and approached the front desk for some tissues, which he transported back to his wife, who remained in the exact same position where he had left her.

He quickly pulled out two tissues from the box and lowered them into her line of sight, and although he feared the rejection of even such a gesture, she took the tissues into her own hand and began blotting her eyes and blowing her nose. Another minute elapsed before she finally picked her head up out of her hands, and Jim could see the blank and flustered face of the wife he had once loved like his very own soul.

"I'm sorry, Jim," she spoke softly as the last of the tears rolled down the outside curves of her cheeks. "It's just so hard. Why'd you have to go and do that, Jimmy? Why? I thought we said we would never, no matter how bad it got."

Jim had no rebuttal. He knew why, and he knew it with all of his being. But he also knew that he could not put words to it without implicating her. And he knew that was a flaw in him which had not been worked out yet. So he kept his mouth shut and continued his silent petition. *Help us, please.*

Another minute or so passed as Penny slowly regained her composure. Finally, she sat bolt upright in her chair and tossed her hair to the side as she looked Jim square in the eyes.

"Is this for real, Jim?" she asked. "Did the President call you, or what actually happened?"

"No, but he wants to meet today," Jim replied, "while we're in DC. That's why I came right over. You know how he is. He wants it done now. He wants that position filled. And he is going to ask me for an answer today. I just know it. I don't know what to do."

"Are you kidding me? You have to take it."

"But you just said—"

"Jim, there may not be hope for us, but there is hope for you. This is what you do. It's what you were born to do. You are a gifted leader, Jim. You're a real jerk. But you have this inside of you—it's always been there."

Jim's mind reeled and rocked. He didn't want to do this alone. He wanted to fight with all of his being for "us," to buck up against the notion that there was no hope—but he knew that now was not that time.

"Penny Lane, you know I love you."

"Cut it out, Jim," Penny said sharply. "You've got to get going and so do I. Let me know how it goes, alright. I'm late to meet Michelle."

With that, Penny stood up abruptly yet without sacrificing any of her usual grace and poise, and she began to traverse the circular lobby toward the front entrance of the hotel without so much as a glance in the direction of her husband. Jim stood to his feet but knew better than to follow his wife out, so he waited for a few minutes feeling as awkward as he looked. The meeting had not gone as he had hoped or expected, but in the end, he felt certain that he had his answer.

"All's well that ends well," he muttered to himself flatly and half-sarcastically as he replayed the conversation over in his mind. He let another moment pass then instinctively hung his head and slowly ambled toward the front door deep in thought, his silhouette shimmying its way through the gold lattice embedded in the black marble floor.

XVIII

"Jim, it's about time you called," Larry's voice boomed on the other end of the phone. "I've been waiting for over an hour. What took you so long? You are going to take the position, right? You would be insane not to, after all you've been through. Come on, let's get this show on the road, old friend. What do you say?"

Jim took a deep breath and swallowed hard. "Yeah, Larry. You call the shots—just tell me what's next. Do they want me to jump through some crazy hoops or what?"

Larry chuckled. "No way. Meet me back at the Jefferson at 11. I'll pick you up, and we'll head over to the White House together. It might be a few hours before we get our meeting, but the sooner we get there the better. In the meantime, I'll work on getting your security clearance. What's your social?"

Jim paused and furrowed his brow as he pulled the phone away from his face.

"I'm just kidding, Jim. Meet me at 11, capiche?"

"Capiche," Jim replied, slightly lackluster. Then he added with a little more enthusiasm and genuine sincerity, "Thanks a lot, Larry."

Jim lowered the phone from his cheek and stared at it blankly in his hand for a few seconds as he continued to process all that was transpiring around him and advancing forward at such a rapid pace. After a moment, he turned on his heels and headed up to his room to freshen up for his meeting with the President of the United States. He had met the President a couple of times during the last campaign season, but they mostly just bantered about the election and keeping Georgia solid red for another two decades. There was a certain ego one had to carry at rallies and fundraisers and all of the unpleasant things that inevitably go into building a successful political career, but Jim had learned long ago to turn it on and off at will.

This meeting would be different though, carrying a much heavier weight and a much more direct purpose. Before, they were connected by party ties and expected to jibe in order to maintain a consistent front for the sake of state and national constituencies, but if this were all to go through, they would need to see eye to eye on a whole host of foreign and domestic policy issues which they had never begun to broach during their brief visits on the campaign trail.

As Jim stood straightening his tie in the mirror, he caught sight of the dark bags that were beginning to form underneath his eyes. He had not slept well since his return stateside. The pressure had been mounting with an impending vote in the Georgia General Assembly on whether to impeach or simply to censure him. Either one would be an embarrassment and leave a ghastly mark on his political rap sheet, and although it was looking like impeachment did not have enough momentum to carry the day, he still felt like he was walking on eggshells all the time.

His home life certainly provided no reprieve, and aside from his evening stroll through the garden, being at home with his family added even more tension to an already intolerably stressful existence. Yet deep down, Jim knew that something had changed in his heart, and that single fact gave him hope.

Sometimes it seemed like only a small glimmer, a tiny fragment of light shining in the faraway distance like a lighthouse emitting its narrow beam from a foreign shore that one had no intention of ever visiting. But it was hope nonetheless, and he found himself guarding the little ember of optimism that had been planted inside of him in a very unexpected place, in a very unlikely way.

It seemed strange to Jim to be rejoicing in the fact that he had finally come to terms with his own brokenness, the ache of time and space which had plagued him since he was a small child. It was all of the same questions that freshman philosophy majors grapple with so proudly, naively thinking they are the first of their species to ponder the ancient enigmas of why and how and when it's all going to end—*if* it's all going to end.

Distorted images of God and the devil had been burned into Jim's psyche from unbearable church services to newspaper comic strips to the religious feuds his uncle Fred was prone to instigate at family gatherings that turned him off to the whole thing. He could never understand why people got so angry talking about a God of love—their words saying one thing, but their faces and body language entirely another. *A picture is worth a thousand words,* Jim told himself. *Maybe they've never considered that, but it applies the same.* He could not seem to shake the thought of all the wars fought in the name of religion, going into battle with a sword in one hand and a holy book in the other. That didn't make any sense to him, but neither did a lot of things. *Of all the crazy running around in this world, that has got to be the craziest,* he thought.

Yet in the midst of it all, Jim had resolved one thing. He didn't know much about God and religion and even love, but he knew that he wanted to be the best man he could be with his remaining days on the earth. He had not articulated the thought in its complete form to anyone and didn't know if he had the verbal wherewithal to do so even if he felt inclined. All he knew was that he had resolved to take things one day at a time, one moment at a time and one person at a time—to love the people in his path each day.

Did the Great Spirit put those people there? Or was it blind chance? Jim pondered as he went about his days. He was not ready to tackle all of the questions that swirled through his mind constantly, but he knew that a phone call from an old acquaintance was about to reshape his entire world. He finished his meticulous grooming session and felt quite pleased with himself. *For an old man, you don't look half bad,* he thought as he eyed himself in the mirror, cocking his head to admire his good side one last time before heading out the door.

His third trip across the Mall that day was by far the least emotional of the lot. In fact, Jim felt a numbness bleeding across his heart that had set in following his conversation with his wife. It was not that he had somehow become indifferent to the out-come of the day's events—it was just that he had completely released himself from any semblance of control over the entire situation.

He had heard stories of this President and knew that anything, literally any possible outcome, could await him at their impending summit. He had determined only to be himself and to be honest—brutally honest at any and all cost. Jim had learned long ago that to acquiesce up front for the sake of winning favor and pleasing the crowd was always a short-term gain, long-term loss.

There is nothing worse than bending your ideals to get into a position that was never a proper fit in the first place, Jim told himself as images of the city flashed before his eyes mingled with the reflections on the glass of the taxi window.

He had not been at the Jefferson but a couple of minutes before Larry pulled up in his black Cadillac DeVille.

"You driving Huey Long around in this thing?" Jim prodded after Larry had rolled down the passenger side window. "I'm for the poor man!" he said in his best Louisiana Cajun accent, lifting both arms in the air and shaking his hands in dramatic fashion.

"Get in the car, you creep," Larry shouted, unable to keep a smile from turning up the edges of his lips. Jim hopped in, and they sped off heading south on 16th Street toward the White House, which was less than a mile away as the crow flies.

"Alright, Jim. Tell me how you're feeling," Larry said over the car radio. "Don't be nervous, this is going to be a breeze. Just tell him that you're thrilled about the position and that you're deeply honored, you know, yadda yadda yadda. Shoot straight, and you'll be fine. How are you feeling, champ? Do you want some water?"

"I'm fine, Larry. Thank you." Jim tried to muster a smile as he spoke but found that his nerves were starting to set in, creating a slight tingling in his fingertips and an uneasiness in his gut. He gently rubbed his hands together as he could feel the perspiration beginning to canvas the thin, clammy skin of his palms. "I feel great. I'm really thankful, Larry," he finally added a bit more assuredly.

Larry drove south on 16th Street for a quarter mile and then turned left onto I Street, followed by a right on 17th.

"Where are we going?" Jim asked casually.

"The New Executive Office Building, "Larry relied. "It's where bottom of the barrel guys like me get to park. But don't worry, the walk's just a block and a half."

After parking the car and being waved through two security checkpoints, Larry led Jim to the main entrance of the West Wing on the north side of the White House. Once inside, they were asked to have a seat across from the receptionist's desk underneath a series of oil paintings in ornate gold frames. Larry continued to reassure Jim about the meeting, but his voice felt distant and cold as the weight and the reality of the moment settled in. After a minute or so, Jim excused himself and stood to his feet as he asked the receptionist where he could find a restroom. She gestured to a spacious hallway behind her desk to the left. "Second door on the right, sir," she said with a polite smile.

Jim's head spun as he crossed the open threshold into the

hallway and fortunately had no trouble finding the men's room. He leaned against the door which swung open easily and nearly stumbled over to the closest sink where he turned on the faucet and cupped his hands to catch the cold streaming water. He splashed his face again and again in hopes that the crippling nerves would leave him and that the pins and needles in his hands and feet would subside.

After about half a dozen repetitions, he turned off the water and allowed the remaining droplets to plunge from the lower rim of his face into the speckled granite sink below. He dried his face and hands with a couple of paper towels and stared intently at his reflection in the mirror. The cool water on his skin had partially revived him, and he felt much steadier and calmer than he had since jumping into the car with Larry at the Jefferson.

Jim closed his eyes and lowered his head in relief that his nerves were returning, and when he opened them again, he caught sight of something in the mirror which made him nearly jump out of his skin. Without a moment of thought, he whipped his body around a full 180 degrees and thrust his back flat against the wall next to the mirror. Standing not 10 feet in front of him was an enormous male lion.

Its coat shone gold and brown all over except for its mane, which had a series of black streaks running through it, and its tail, which sported a small, black tuft of fur on the tip. The lion stood about three and half feet tall and must have weighed 400 pounds. Its strong, lean muscles could be seen clearly underneath its short coat, instantly arousing in Jim the awareness that his life could be over in a moment's time if this encounter were to go awry.

"Why is it," Jim began between heaving breaths, "that you always feel like you have to scare the life out of me—literally?" He paused to catch his breath. "I mean, I'm no good to you dead. Just keep that in mind, big fella."

The lion's eyes twinkled as it swished its long tail back and forth, back and forth. It appeared to be in no sort of hurry at all, exuding a patient strength which simultaneously evoked both a sense of fear and awe. Yet at the very same moment, Jim experienced a sense of stillness deep inside which produced in him the notion that it would be impossible to feel truly frightened in this place. Aside from the initial jolt, the familiar peace and complete serenity of the Great Spirit had enveloped him the first moment he saw the lion face to face, melting away all discomfort and tension in his body from head to toe.

Even his mind had been washed with peace, and he could instantly think clearly, which stood in stark contrast to the rollercoaster of thoughts and emotions he had been experiencing for most of the day. He took a deep, long inhale as he felt his lungs expanding and his chest and shoulders rising, which consequentially lifted his head and made him realize that his eyes had been fixed on the ground since his meeting with his wife about an hour prior.

"Jim," the lion half roared and half spoke, making the hairs on the back of Jim's neck stand on end. "Lift up your head and stand up like a man."

Jim instantly straightened up like an arrow and clamored to

attention, reassembling a new recruit at basic training trying to appease his overbearing drill sergeant.

"You have no reason to cast your gaze to the ground any longer," the majestic beast continued. "You have turned away from your crooked path and have returned to the way of life. You must not carry your past failures into your present season and darken it with an evil which does not belong there. Do these words ring true?"

"Yes," Jim managed to respond in a voice no louder than a faint whisper. "Yes, they do."

"Good. It's mighty fine to lay eyes on you, Jim Hamilton. Do you know who I am or what I represent?"

Jim stood frozen stiff and silent, still recovering from the lion's initial roar, which had sent shock waves through his body and had touched his spirit in a way that he had no words to describe.

"My name is Mosaddegh, and I am an Asiatic lion, the national animal of Iran. Jim, what do you know about Mohammad Mosaddegh?"

"Hold on," Jim rebutted, drawing another long, deep breath. "I know we're going to jump right in, but, but, I just need a second to—"

"Catch your breath?" the lion interrupted. Without missing a beat, the massive animal reared back its head slightly, braced its front and hind legs, and then released a breath so mighty and so powerful that it felt like a gust of gale force wind, which may very well have toppled Jim over if he had not been propped up against the bathroom wall.

Instantly, a tranquility that Jim could not describe overtook his being, and he began laughing as wave after wave of pure giddiness washed over him. Jim closed his eyes, and he could see the swing set at the park around the corner from his childhood home where he would go and fly through the air for hours and hours to get away from the pressure and the stress and the constant demands of his home and his overbearing father. He could see the ground rhythmically swaying beneath him in an elliptical pattern as the trees rose and fell, rose and fell, their leaves shimmering like gold as both he and they bathed in the warm sunlight.

For several minutes, Jim forgot where he was and even who he was in a sense—or who he had become—and all he could fit into his conscious mind at that moment in time was the little boy, his former self, still pure and innocent from the defilements of this world, not perfect as anyone who has ever spent more than a few minutes with little boys can attest, but simple and straightforward and not yet overtaken by the lusts of life and romance, wealth and power.

At first, he basked in the ecstatic joy of the memory itself, in the weightlessness that that simple season of life brought to his remembrance. But before long, he began to mourn. He mourned the loss of that little boy, the loss of his capacity for love and for forgiveness and for simple kindness, not that those were always his first instinct—in fact, far from it. Yet nothing systematic had at that point crept into his life to undermine those precious virtues as had been the case for so many decades of his adult life, his quest for self-advancement trumping the most basic awareness of the needs of those around him. Instantly, his laughter faded into quiet tears, and his mind became clouded with a feeling of utter darkness and despair.

"Jim," the lion's voice rang out urgently, resonating off the walls and the floor and the ceiling with a mighty echo that awoke Jim like a resounding thunder clap and thrust him back into the present moment. "Do not allow your mind to go there. You have been given this picture for reminiscence, not for regret. You could never have held on to that season of your life—no one can nor are they meant to. You must learn to enjoy what is set before you without holding on so tightly."

"But I've always held on tightly," Jim responded, pulling himself together. "To everything. It's how I was raised. Don't let anything go, not 'til you've squeezed the life out of it, that is."

"Jim, life isn't about squeezing everything to the last drop. Have you ever thought about leaving a little something for those who come behind you?"

The lion's words instantly reminded Jim of a man his father used to do business with who would always say, "Mr. Hamilton, there's enough room in this deal for everyone to make a buck. And don't forget to leave a little room for the next guy." Jim remembered his father laughing off the remarks. "The next guy?" he would say mockingly to Jim after their meetings. "Let him make his own buck."

"Why do you suppose," the lion probed further, "that people hold on so tightly? To their time, their possessions, their traditions—to their way of seeing the world?"

Jim paused for a moment to think. "Well, I suppose it is connected to fear. They are afraid they will lose what they have, that they will lose their comfort, their security, or even sometimes their entire way of life."

"And what is fear? Or rather, what is it the lack of?"

"Fear," he began contemplatively, "is the lack of trust. If you don't trust that tomorrow will bring good things, you are more likely to hold on to what you have today."

"Exactly," the lion roared with a hint of a smile. "Fear is the absence of trust just like cold is the absence of heat. It doesn't exist on its own. Those who know how to trust have a much easier time releasing what they have and letting go."

"But how can we trust in anything?" Jim interrupted. "That doesn't make any sense. Nobody knows what the future will bring."

"You do believe in the invisible hand don't you?"

"If you are referring to Adam Smith's economic theory, then yes. But what does that have to do with anything?"

"Well, if you believe that the market is guided by an invisible driving force which ultimately works all of the gazillions of individual choices made on a daily basis together for the greater good of society and mankind, then what makes you think that it's not true for the rest of life as well? And what makes you think that just because you can't see it that it's random?"

"What exactly are you angling at?"

"The Great Spirit, Jim." Mosaddegh lifted his head as he spoke, his mane shimmering gold and black. "Just think about all the laws of nature, those discovered by Newton and Einstein and Lavoisier. How can you believe in all of these natural laws but never consider who made them or who enforces them? There are 100 trillion cells in your body all working together just so you can stand here and take your next breath. There are 100 billion neurons in your brain each sending dozens of signals per second so you can have this conversation. You see the invisible hand at work in market forces, but you refuse to see it in the realm of physics and quantum mechanics, biology and chemistry. Just as your heart constantly pumps blood to your body whether you are aware of it or not, the Great Spirit is always behind the scenes orchestrating all things together for the good of humanity—whether people believe it or not."

"But how can you say that the Great Spirit is guiding the affairs of mankind for the greater good while bloody wars rage on and global warming marches steadily forward and while thousands of people die every day from malnutrition?"

"These are all man-made evils, Jim. The Great Spirit has given human beings the freedom to choose, to map out their own future and destiny. And for better or worse, you are all left to face the consequences of your actions, both individually and collectively. Seventy percent of all global carbon emissions are produced by just 100 corporations. Yet you continue to fill up your gas tank at their stations and buy your electricity from them. There is enough food produced in the world to feed one and a half times the total human population. Yet Americans waste 40% of the food they produce. And as for war. What do you expect when your nation spends close to a trillion dollars on war each year? And when you teach your children to cheer for fighter jets when they fly overhead, armed to the teeth with lethal bombs and missiles? Every action, no matter how small, has a consequence. Whatever you tolerate in this life will ultimately become your reality."

"But we have no other choice," Jim responded with a hint of exasperation in his voice. "People have to work and eat and live. And what say do 99% of Americans have on carbon emissions or the military budget? Our politicians are all beholden to corporations and their interests, not the interests of the people—on both sides of the aisle. Trust me, I would know. Let's face it, we're stuck."

"Yes, but look at how these domestic and global situations are awakening the conscience of your nation like never before. There is a groundswell of intolerance for the status quo and for the corporate-driven political oligarchy that has cemented its power in your nation's capital. The youth are reading and asking and probing like never before. They will not be satisfied with the rote answers that were fed to your generation. They have too much access to information—the raw, real truth. And they are determined to learn from your history to avoid repeating it. The Great Spirit is breathing on this generation for change. Real change. Revolutionary change. You must learn to trust that good is coming even when you can't see it."

Jim rubbed the back of his neck with his hand and stared off at the corner of the ceiling as he mulled over this thought.

"Which brings me, Jim, back to Iran. The time is short, and we have a lot to cover. So tell me please, what do you know about Mohammad Mosaddegh?"

"Hmm," Jim took a moment to switch gears. "Let's see. Mosaddegh was the Prime Minister of Iran. Which was essentially the head of state, but he still answered to the Shah. In 1953, he was overthrown by a coup orchestrated by the CIA and the British MI6, after trying to nationalize Iranian oil. Is that where you're going with this? The oil connection?"

"Sort of. Oil plays a big part. Why else would major world powers be fighting bloody wars in the middle of the desert? Think about it, Jim. If there were no oil in the Middle East, it would be just like Africa. Exploitation, yes. But endless global wars? No way. Mosaddegh was overthrown because of the oil. Do you remember the British corporation behind the coop?"

"Of course, it was BP, or back then the Anglo-Persian Oil Company. Under their agreements, Iran only got 16% of the profits of the sale of their oil, and they were sick of it. Especially since the US cut a deal with Saudi Arabia in 1950 to split profits 50-50. The British refused to budge on the percentages, so a popular movement arose in Iran to nationalize the whole industry, which Mosaddegh spearheaded. Britain appealed to the US for help, and the coup was born."

"Did it succeed?" Mosaddegh asked.

"Well, it lasted longer than the coup against Chávez, that's for sure. The new government established by the United States and Britain basically stood for 25 years until the Iranian Revolution in 1979."

"And what did the US have to gain in all of this?"

"Immediately after the coup," Jim continued, "the new Prime

Minister renegotiated Iran's oil concessions with both the US and Britain, and the US got a big cut. So the $6 million that the CIA spent on the coup came back to them in a big way, and they used the ongoing oil revenue to support the Iranian government for the next two and half decades, fostering a strong allegiance all the way up to the 1979 revolution."

"Tell me, Jim, what you know about the Iranian Revolution?"

"I mean, it was a total step backwards for the country—the government in the hands of religious zealots, freedom of speech and religion thrown out the window, women relegated to second class citizens and forced to wear veils in public at all times. It was a complete rejection of modern progress and democracy. Even the Ayatollah himself said that Iran would no longer be considered a democracy and began repressing opposition parties and media outlets. Dissidents were imprisoned, tortured and often killed. It set Iran on a crash course, especially with the West, really up to this day."

"Jim, you are talking about the effects of the revolution. But what about the causes of it?"

Jim opened his mouth to speak and then paused. He reflected for a moment, averting his gaze to gather his thoughts.

"I suppose," Jim began slowly, choosing his words carefully, "that the causes were the same as all populist revolutions. The people were dissatisfied with their leadership and representation, tired of not getting their fair share of the nation's wealth and resources, and done listening to the same old story told over and over by the ruling class about change that never actually comes."

"Precisely. And let me ask you a question. If it was a proven fact that on November 22, 1963, your beloved president John F. Kennedy had been assassinated by a hit man hired by the Iranian government, do you think that memory would ever be erased from your mind?"

"Of course not," Jim said flatly, picturing exactly where he was in the back seat of his mother's Plymouth Belvedere when the news came over the car radio that JFK had been shot.

"What people outside of Iran fail to realize," the massive lion began again, "about the Iranian Revolution is the aching void that the 1953 coup against Mosaddegh left, not just in the nation at a macro level, but in the hearts of its citizens. They were so close to revolution then, under a leader who truly represented the cause and plight of the people—instituting land reforms, sick pay for factory workers, unemployment compensation, and a real plan to use oil revenue to fight poverty and disease.

"To have such a strong popular movement," Mosaddegh continued, "which itself was a boiling pot from decades of government repression, subverted by Western intervention in a matter of four days was a crushing blow to the people of Iran. The coup took less than a week to carry out, but it stuck in the minds of the people for the next 25 years.

"As a result, the Iranian Revolution was like no other revolution in modern history. There was no pressing military conflict, no spiraling national debt, people weren't starving in the streets. But Iranians remembered the coup, and they resented the Shah, who the United States and Britain reinstated in its wake. For 25 years, the Shah upheld the lopsided oil concessions that had been negotiated by the crony government that the CIA propped up following Mosaddegh's overthrow.

"The CIA also helped the Shah create a secret police force called the SAVAK, which he used to torture and execute thousands of political prisoners in utterly inhumane ways. At the same time, the Shah flaunted the extreme opulence that his relationship with the US afforded him at the expense of his own people. Ultimately, Iranians longed to get out from underneath a rulership that sided with the interests of Western power, wealth and influence over the welfare of its own citizens again and again."

"But it was a religious movement," Jim rebutted. "The goal wasn't the welfare of the people—it was to make Islam the state religion. Just look at the repression now. "

"Although religion played an important role in the revolution," Mosaddegh replied, "as it does in all of Iranian culture, the secular influences cannot be underplayed. Crippling strikes in government industries and massive demonstrations in the streets organized by the labor movement, Marxists and student organizations ground the Iranian economy to a complete halt. Even in the face of gunfire, with thousands of unarmed protestors killed by national military forces, the people marched on.

"What your history-amnesia prone media outlets refuse to acknowledge," the great lion went on, "is how socialist and communist ideology nearly always arises as a response to corrupt capitalism connected to some form of either colonialism or imperialism. Remember, there is no such thing as a truly free market. The rules must be set by someone, whoever holds the seats of power, and it is those rules which will always dictate the winners and the losers. And when people lose big enough and stay in poverty long enough despite working their fingers to the bone, they will always seek an alternative route to ensure that their children and grandchildren have a chance at a better life.

"All of the elements of the Iranian Revolution you mentioned which rubbed you the wrong way emerged after the dust had settled and Ayatollah Ruhollah Khomeini had managed to consolidate power. If the US had kept its hands out of the dispute with Britain over oil concessions in the first place, perhaps Mosaddegh's revolution would have taken root and focused on empowering the poor rather than a complete religious overhaul of the government into a virulently anti-Western theocracy."

"Sure, hindsight is 20/20," Jim responded. "How could they have known what the results were going to be 25 years down the line?"

"What you have to be willing to see," answered Mosaddegh, "is that everywhere on the map where America, or any other imperial power for that matter, asserts its political and economic dominance through military force, inevitable disastrous repercussions are bound to follow. You think the Iranian Revolution was bad? Look at the rise of Isis after 20 years of shelling Iraq. Or even worse, the rise of Pol Pot after your nation mercilessly carpet-bombed Cambodia toward the end of the Vietnam War.

"From 1969 to 1973, the US military dropped more than

2.5 million tons of bombs across the countryside of Cambodia in order to destroy North Vietnamese military bases and to disrupt their supply routes. The United States never even declared war on Cambodia, yet the relentless bombing killed hundreds of thousands of civilians and left over two million people homeless. The bombings were used by Pol Pot to radicalize a war-torn nation, leading to the rise of his Khmer Rouge and allowing the regime to purge the nation of all political moderates. From 1975 to 1979, an estimated 1.5 to 2 million people died at his hands from execution, forced labor, starvation and disease.

"Although your top government officials had detailed knowledge of the genocide, they did nothing to stop it. And when Vietnam invaded Cambodia in 1979, finally toppling the regime and ending the nightmare, the United States supported Khmer Rouge guerillas against Vietnamese forces in order to continue to isolate Vietnam on the world stage. The United States supported the Khmer Rouge guerillas throughout the 1980s and refused to acknowledge the Cambodian Genocide until 1997, allowing Pol Pot to evade capture until 1998.

"Or look at Afghanistan. In July of 2000, the Taliban collaborated with the UN to completely eradicate heroin production in the country. They implemented a ban on opium farming and reduced the amount of opium produced in Taliban areas by 99%—at a time when Afghanistan supplied three quarters of the world's illicit heroin. The ban was short lived as the Taliban was deposed from power in 2002 because of the US invasion, leading to an enormous resurgence in opium farming nationwide.

"Almost 20 years of incessant war later, Afghanistan is turning out bumper crops of opium, the only thing for poor farmers to grow in a conflict-torn country, producing over 90% of the world's illicit heroin and creating a drug epidemic that is being felt the world over, including on your very own shores. And what is your government's response to the crisis? More bombs. The US dropped nearly 1,000 bombs on Afghanistan in September 2019 alone—*this year*, Jim—18 years after the start of this endless war. And the targets? Drug labs, many of which are nothing more than mud huts and farm houses. Your military is trying to destroy the very thing the Taliban willingly destroyed two decades ago—and that your illegal war resurrected. And what's the kicker? The Taliban controls more territory now than they did when the US invasion began in 2001.

"Jim, when your nation drops bombs, you call it democracy and freedom. When other nations drop bombs, you call it communism and terrorism. But neither is the truth. It's all war— just war, death and destruction. The United States engages mostly in traditional warfare because you have the resources to do it. So how do poor populations fight back? They make homemade bombs and IEDs and fly planes into buildings. It's nothing more than guerilla warfare. When your beloved Francis Marion engaged in guerilla warfare against the British, you called him a hero. But when disgruntled Iraqi youth plant roadside bombs, you call them monsters. History is always written by the victors."

Mosaddegh caught eyes with Jim, who paused for a moment before responding. "I just don't see," Jim began thoughtfully, "why the Great Spirit would advocate for a government that is so repressive to women and minorities. At least in America, we can speak and dress and worship freely. It just doesn't seem at all consistent."

"Don't forget, Jim," Mosaddegh responded with a certain gentleness in his tone, "that the rights you enjoy today were denied to women and minorities for centuries in your nation. The slaves who were captured and forcefully brought to your shores enjoyed no freedoms whatsoever and were actually considered by your Constitution to be only three-fifths of a human being, despite making up approximately 20% of the population at the time of your nation's birth. Legalized repression of the black community continued for another century after the Civil War through extremely socially and politically restrictive Jim Crow laws, and it continues to be felt through disparities in policing and criminal justice to this day.

"The Native American people have also been consistently targeted and repressed since your nation's colonial era. Native Americans born in the United States were not considered US citizens until 1924 and were not guaranteed the right to vote in every state until 1962. In 1830, the United States government forced all Native Americans to move west of the Mississippi River with the passage of the Indian Removal Act, and in 1883, Native American religion was made illegal with the Code of Indian Offenses, punishing traditional dances and feasts with imprisonment or withholding food rations. Beginning in 1879, the US government forcefully removed tens of thousands of Native American children from their families in order to attend boarding schools designed to assimilate them into American culture, a practice which continued all the way up to the 1970s. The stated purpose of the schools was to 'Kill the Indian, Save the Man.'"

"You're pretty good at dredging up the dirt of American History," Jim answered sharply, "but at least we've corrected those mistakes—it was called the Civil Rights Movement. We have come a long, long way since the founding of this nation."

Mosaddegh drew a deep breath that sounded like a muffled sigh. "Jim, I'm not sure about the 'we' that you're referring to, but white governors like yourself from the Solid South didn't come out of the Civil Rights era with too great of a track record, nor did the white community at large. If you will remember, the movement was violently repressed by the government and resisted by virtually everyone in the white community, from politicians and business owners to housewives and clergymen. Peaceful, non-violent demonstrations were met again and again with water hoses, police dogs, billy clubs and mass arrests. Children as young as nine years old were arrested and put in jail for marching silently and holding signs.

"The FBI infiltrated every part of the movement," the lion continued, "targeting activists and leaders through constant surveillance, harassment, imprisonment, false media reports, violence and even assassination. A 1976 report produced by a US Senate committee revealed that only a small percentage of FBI efforts were focused on solving crime while the vast majority was spent targeting domestic political organizations, those fighting for rights they were supposedly guaranteed under the US Constitution.

"This trend of FBI infiltration and disruption continues to this day with movements such as Occupy Wall Street and Black Lives Matter. But as NSA whistleblower Edward Snowden has shown the whole world, the United States government is not just spying on a handful of activists anymore—they are constantly collecting information on anyone and everyone. There is no such thing as privacy today in America.

"Your people talk about the Civil Rights Movement like it was the end of all injustice in your nation. Yet the most disturbing and repressive systems in the United States since slavery—the War on Drugs and mass incarceration—actually arose from it, just as Jim Crow rose out of the ashes of Reconstruction following the Civil War. The overwhelming American response to legislated desegregation in the 1950s and 60s was to immediately resegregate, through white flight in the South and through redlining and restrictive covenants in the Northeast, Midwest and West. Along with the rise of government project housing, these trends left the poor black community more segregated and disconnected from the white middle and upper class than it had ever been before.

"With all connections severed to the thriving, mostly-white economic system, the only economy available in most poor black neighborhoods was the illegal drug trade. It was not a question of morality, but one of survival. Yet your government's response was tragic. Rather than economic intervention or even a drug rehabilitation initiative, poor black communities across the country were ravaged by a military-style police invasion.

"Kids were stopped and frisked on their way to school. SWAT teams kicked down doors. Black males disappeared from their communities en masse—locked up and forgotten. Instead of cops and robbers, little kids played cops and drug dealers in the streets. Zero tolerance drug policies that sounded great in the halls of Washington, DC tore the black community apart at the seams and ended all hopes of Martin Luther King, Jr's dream to let freedom ring for all races and classes in America.

"When Nixon declared a nationwide War on Drugs in 1971, there were less than 350,000 total inmates behind bars in the US. Today, there are nearly 2.3 million people living out the American Dream in six by eight foot cages, giving the United States the highest incarceration rate of any nation in the world. In the half century prior to the 1970s, the male incarceration rate remained incredibly steady at 0.2%. By 1986, it had doubled to 0.4%, and by 1996, it had doubled again to 0.8%. By 2008, it had reached its historic high of 0.95%, which means that essentially one out of every 100 males in the United States were locked behind bars, as opposed to one in 500 prior to the War on Drugs.

"The racial outcomes are similarly undeniable. To this day, black men are six times more likely to be incarcerated in the US than their white counterparts, and one in three can expect to go to jail at some point in their lifetime. *One in three.* That's an albatross they will wear around their necks for the rest of their lives, garnering legalized discrimination in the realms of employment, housing, education, public assistance and even voting rights in many states."

"And whose fault is that?" Jim interrupted hotly. "If you break the law, you should expect to go to jail. Nobody's forcing these people to sell drugs."

"And you've never broken the law?" the great lion replied, shaking its head slightly and giving Jim a grave look. "Have you ever thought about why your frat house was never raided by a SWAT team? There were enough drugs in there to fly a rocket to the moon. And why do you think it took 100 times as much powder cocaine to trigger the same mandatory minimum five-year federal prison sentence as five grams of crack cocaine? That law didn't fall out of the sky—someone had to write it. And let me assure you, not one of the sponsors of that legislation had ever been faced with the decision to sell drugs or to go hungry. Laws are established just like markets are, Jim. There are winners, and there are losers.

"If you look at the past half century," Mosaddegh went on, "there has been no significant change in the crime rate in America, just a drastic shift in drug laws and sentencing. Technically, anyone who breaks the law is a criminal. But you're not a criminal in the eyes of the state until you have been caught and convicted. Just look at Prohibition. One day, alcohol use and distribution was perfectly legal—the next, it wasn't. Overnight, a massive black market was created by one law that led to the deaths of around 10,000 people before it was repealed. But because the middle and upper class white communities were the ones affected by Prohibition, it only lasted 13 years. The War on Drugs, which has primarily affected poor black (and more recently Hispanic) communities, has been raging on for four decades with no end in sight.

"Jim, it's very hard for you as a white male to understand the plight of the black community in America, or that of any minority community in any nation—including Iran. Iranian Shiite men enjoy tremendous social and political freedom in their nation as the ethnic majority. It would be hard even for them to truly understand the plight of women in their nation, who in 1936 were totally banned from wearing veils, or hijabs, and in 1983 were forced to wear them at all times. Or the struggle for equal rights under the law by Iranian Sunnis, who make up around five to ten percent of the population and who face constant persecution and repression because of their faith.

"Although blacks and whites in America use illegal drugs at completely comparable rates, the affluent white community has not been affected by the War on Drugs—because it wasn't a war on drugs at all. It was yet another tool of legalized repression employed against the black community. One of Nixon's top advisors, John Ehrlichman, later admitted that the primary impetus for the War of Drugs was to create a way to legally target and villainize hippies, who opposed the war in Vietnam, and blacks, who opposed him politically.

"Just think about it. In 1971, the year that Nixon declared that drug abuse was 'public enemy number one,' there were only approximately 5,000 drug overdose deaths in the US. That same year, the Bangladesh genocide raged on with estimates of the death toll ranging from hundreds of thousands to 3 million people slaughtered at the hands of the Pakistani military over a nine month period. Not only did Nixon chose not to intervene on behalf of the Bangladeshi people, his administration continued to provide US arms to Pakistan even after receiving reports of the genocide, suppressing the reports and refusing to condemn Yahya Khan, the President of Pakistan, since he was a close Cold War ally."

"There you go again," Jim broke in sharply, "dredging up the past. Listen, I know it's terrible, I really do get it. But what does this have to do with anything?"

"Jim," Mosaddegh replied with patience in his deep voice, "the past is the lens through which we must see the present and our most effective tool for navigating the future. Otherwise, we will inevitably fall into the same destructive patterns as those who have come before us. My point is this. In 1971, more than 25,000 people were killed by drunk drivers in the US, five times as many as those who died from drug overdose. But neither alcohol nor genocide made it to the top of Nixon's list. Instead, he ignored a real international crisis to create a fabricated one, a new American war waged against a new American enemy—drugs—to go down in history alongside communism and terrorism as the three most repressive, fear-based and propaganda-driven offenses in your nation's history.

"The War on Drugs, just as intended, has been used by your government as a tool of violent repression against the black and Hispanic communities domestically, but also against Mexicans and Colombians and countless other people groups and nations worldwide. There really isn't much difference between locking up a black man in inner city Detroit for selling drugs and bombing an Afghan farmer in Kabul for growing opium. Both are simply utilizing the only economy available to them in order to survive.

"Yet the insidious part of both scenarios is how US intervention actually created the economic deserts which allowed the illegal drug trade to thrive in the first place—through redlining in Detroit and through decades of war in Afghanistan—and then cracked down on those same communities with harsh drug policies and enforcement. Poverty breeds illegal economies, and illegal economies attract violence. Yet rather than addressing the economic root of impoverished communities, we harshly penalize the symptoms. It's the same vicious cycle again and again.

"American repression is not overt like you see in a theocracy such as Iran, but ask anyone who has ever taken a hard stance opposing US economic interests, either domestically or globally, and they will tell you—not only is it very real, but it's swift and more powerful than you can imagine. Just ask Fred Hampton or any of the Civil Rights leaders who laid down their lives to end legalized segregation. Or more recently, Evo Morales. In 2006 as the newly elected President of Bolivia, Morales nationalized his country's oil and gas industries on his 100th day in office and has used the revenue to help the poor ever since. Sound familiar? That was the day he signed his own death warrant. You saw it in the news just last week. They said it wasn't a coup, that he 'resigned.' Well, of course he resigned.

You would too if your uniformed generals gave you an ultimatum. Military leaders forcing a democratically elected president to resign—if that's not a coup, then what is? Fortunately, he was ousted without having to lose his life. But from the very start, the clock is ticking on guys like him.

"This is not a conversation about the past, Jim. It's the present day reality of life on planet Earth. I have shown you the historic trends so that you can accurately decipher the events swirling around you today—and to open your eyes to the reality that the United States of America has become the most repressive force on the face of the earth."

"Are you totally mad?" Jim interrupted scoffingly. "How on earth can you say that the United States is more repressive than communist nations like China and Russia, and the worst of them all, North Korea?"

"Yes, Jim, you are right about North Korea," Mosaddegh responded with an evenness in his voice, "but let me explain my point. North Korea has the most repressive *culture* by far of any nation in the world and perhaps in the history of the world. The central governments of Russia and China both maintain elements of strong social, political and religious repression, far worse than what is seen in the United States domestically.

"But the difference is that the repression of all three of these nations is mostly limited to the citizens of those nations. North Korea has zero foreign military presence, and China didn't have a single foreign military base until 2017, when they opened an army base in Djibouti. Prior to the end of the Cold War in 1991, the Soviet Union did have a large repressive footprint, but today

Russia, the largest republic of the USSR, operates only roughly 20 foreign military bases worldwide. The United States, on the other hand, has over 800 military bases located in 80 nations around the world. There is simply no comparison in history to the United States' military occupation of the planet—not even Rome came close.

"Just think about the signal that such a global military presence sends to the rest of the world. Foreign bases don't exist to protect the lives of US citizens. You have thousands of bases right here at home to do that. China has no trouble defending its sovereign border with no foreign military presence and more than four times your population. The purpose of a massive foreign *military* infrastructure is not to protect life, but to protect a massive foreign *economic* infrastructure, the global investments of US multinational corporations and the tiny percentage of your citizens who own large stakes in them. Your foreign military hubs act as an ever-present reminder that the US military is always within striking distance of any factory, any pipeline, any oil refinery, any plantation—any target whatsoever.

"At any given time, anywhere around the globe, anyone or anything that threatens US economic interests had better beware. And the lengths your nation is willing to go have already been recorded in the bloody annuls of history—wars, coups, assassinations, sanctions, financial strangulation, misinformation campaigns and the propping up of some of the most brutal and inhumane regimes around the world, names that would send chills down your spine.

"Many of the Central and South American war criminals of the 20th century, including El Salvadoran death-squad organizer, Roberto D'Aubuisson, were not only backed by the US, they were trained at the School of the Americas in Fort Benning, Georgia. More than 80,000 Latin American military and police officers have been educated at the school, which still operates to this day as the Western Hemisphere Institute for Security Cooperation, historically advocating untenable practices such as torture, execution, blackmail, extortion and targeting civilian populations. In El Salvador alone, D'Aubuisson and the death squads were responsible for 40,000 political murders in the early 1980s—in a nation with only 4.5 million people at the time.

"The reality is that the United States has a double standard when it comes to its ideals of freedom and democracy. And it's not just Latin America. Your nation continues to support and even install repressive regimes across the globe that your people wouldn't tolerate for one minute stateside. Consider for a moment the type of human being who would be willing to stage a coup and overthrow their democratically elected president for a bribe. You're not talking salt of the earth people, Jim. Yet as long as they are willing to carry out your nation's global economic agenda, blatant corruption and even sheer brutality can and will be overlooked.

Your nation's long history of oppression and repression did not just suddenly end with the Civil Rights Movement—it merely got shipped overseas. So while your government delivers one brand of freedom and democracy to your 325 million citizens, it's a very different model that your State Department is hawking for the rest of the 7.8 billion people alive on the face of the earth. Do you understand how frightening and unsettling it is to know that at any moment, your government and your economy and even your entire way of life could be thrown into complete upheaval for the crime of crossing the big, bad US of A? That, Jim, is repression. It keeps global leaders in line with your agenda, most of the time without ever having to fire a shot—yet it will never be felt by the vast majority of your citizens."

"Give me just one good example," Jim challenged him, "and not another history lesson. A *current* example."

"Jim, when the power goes out at the polling center for 24 hours like it did two years ago in the middle of the Honduran national election and the US-backed candidate, Juan Orlando Hernández, suddenly surges forward to overcome a quote insurmountable lead and take the victory, it doesn't take a blood hound to smell a rat. Said they 'recounted the rural vote.' Everyone in the country and even the whole region knows that it was rigged, but what can they do about it? All they want is the freedom to democratically elect their own leaders, but who in the international community is willing to go to bat against the US and risk their neck for little old Honduras? This came only eight years after a 2009 military coup ousting democratically elected President Manuel Zelaya and sending the nation into a spiral of violence and economic stagnation. Yet ironically the refugees fleeing the violence and repression in migrant caravans have been denied political asylum at the US border.

"This is just a tiny drop in the bucket of the everyday reality in a world under US hegemony. Nobody is even allowed to hold a fair election anymore. Democracy is under fire from its supposed epicenter. Your citizens love to tout America as a free nation. Well, it's the only free nation left on the planet. As they say, freedom is not free—and yours comes at the expense of the rest of the world."

Jim stood internalizing these words as the fierce eyes of the lion glowed like flames of fire, penetrating into the depths of his heart. "But," he began and then paused for a moment to gather his thoughts. "How can this sort of thing happen right underneath our noses, and no one is even crying foul?"

"Oh, they are," Mosaddegh replied. "Believe me, they are. But what are the chances that those voices ever reach your ears? You have to remember that the corporate media oligopoly is 100% complicit and one of the primary tools employed to keep the American public completely in the dark about what the US empire is doing all over the world. While they shamefully twist the true narrative of virtually all of your foreign involvement around the globe, their greatest and most powerful tool is to simply distract the masses, currently with an endless charade of political antics and drama right here in Washington, DC. All the while, real bombs are falling and real coups are happening and real outcries about real injustices are being silenced—and as a result, real people are suffering all over the world. Covering up America's covert wars and global military coercion seems to be the only point of total bipartisan convergence in your otherwise polarized national media.

"Back to your original question, Jim. The Great Spirit is not advocating for Iran's government or any other government of any other nation on the face of the earth. But make no mistake, the Great Spirit is advocating for the Iranian people. And all people everywhere. Especially those whose lives are affected by greed-driven intervention and oppression. When one people takes it upon themselves to dominate another people, the heart of the Great Spirit is moved.

"The United States' interference in the affairs of the sovereign nation of Iran since the 1950s has caused a tremendous amount of suffering to the Iranian people. It has never for a moment been about ending repression or advancing freedom and democracy. Or about weapons of mass destruction—you'd think your people would have learned the sound of that dog whistle from your illegal invasion of Iraq.

"It all started with oil, backing BP's coup and propping up the Shah for 25 years, and it's still all about oil, four decades after the Revolution in 1979 completely ousted all Western oil companies from Iran. Predictably one year after the nationalization of Iran's oil, the United States backed Iraqi forces in their 1980 invasion of Iran, providing weapons, funding and intelligence to Iraq for nearly a decade until the war's end in 1988. The US even provided biological agents such as anthrax and bubonic plague, which Saddam Hussein used to slaughter citizens and soldiers alike, in violation of international law.

"Although your nation's top decision makers were fully aware of Iraq's use of chemical weapons beginning in 1983, they turned a blind eye for the next five years leading to the agonizing deaths of 50,000 to 100,000 Iranians—anything to avoid the spread of the Islamic Revolution, which in their minds posed a threat to oil supplies in the entire Gulf region. Ironically, they cited Saddam's used of these same chemical weapons to justify your unlawful war against Iraq in 2003.

"Yet far more devastating than your government's support of the Iran-Iraq War have been the crippling sanctions that your State Department has employed against Iran, beginning in 1979 and continuing to this day, as well as many forms of cyber and financial warfare. These tactics tend to hurt the most vulnerable in the population, specifically children, the elderly and those with chronic medical conditions.

"In 2018, the US government began a 'maximum pressure' campaign, imposing economy-wide sanctions and a complete financial blockade designed to choke out all oil exports and to bring the Iranian economy to a screeching halt. Although the United Nations has spoken out against the sanctions, declaring them unjust and harmful, the US State Department has shown no signs of backing down. With such a complete stranglehold on the international financial system, the US government is accountable to no one. Meanwhile, with no end in sight, the sanctions are causing hyperinflation, driving millions of people into poverty, and preventing the Iranian people from getting the basic necessities of life—food, medicine and even paper and ink for print newspapers.

"The nonstop US offensive against Iran over the past four decades sends a bleak signal to countries like Venezuela and Bolivia, and frankly to the rest of the world, that the United

States will not let up until it achieves full international cooperation with its global economic agenda. To say that Iran is a threat to US national security, which is the justification for the sanctions, is a total farce. The last time Iran invaded another nation was in 1738. The United States can't seem to go a couple of years without declaring war on someone or attempting to overthrow a sovereign government."

"Hold on a second," Jim interjected. "Just because they don't go around crossing borders doesn't mean they aren't a threat. Iran is the biggest sponsor of state terrorism in the world. Plus, they are enriching Uranium as we speak. How can you say *that* doesn't pose a threat to US security?"

"Jim, the United States has more than 4,000 nuclear weapons, and Israel has as estimated 80 or 90. Do you know how many Iran has? Zero. The Western media has been sounding the alarm on an Iranian nuclear threat since the mid-1980s, but don't you think it's a bit ironic for a nation with thousands of armed nuclear warheads to accuse a nation that doesn't have a single one of being 'an imminent nuclear threat' for more than three decades and running?

"And don't you also think it might not be a coincidence," Mosaddegh continued, "that your media began floating the idea of a nuclear threat just a few years after the Revolution and the nationalization of the oil and the beginning of the sanctions? Remember the allegation that your State Department used to pry its way into Iraq after 9/11? Weapons of mass destruction. There were never any weapons of mass destruction in Iraq and everyone who was anyone knew it, but when such strong allegations are repeated over and over again by 'trusted' media outlets, it eventually wears down public resistance to illegal intervention and even full-blown war—regardless of whether the accusations turn out to be true or not. It's precisely the same strategy with the nuclear threat in Iran.

"All of the fearmongering over the Iranian nuclear threat is even more obscured by the fact that the Supreme Leader of Iran, Ayatollah Ali Khamenei, issued an official fatwa, or Islamic law, against the development or use of nuclear weapons in the late 1990s that stands to this day. As you have pointed out, Iran is a nation which follows its Islamic law to the tee. If they follow their fatwa about nuclear weapons half as fervently as they do the fatwa about head coverings, your nation has absolutely nothing to worry about.

"As for Iran's sponsorship of terrorism, there is just one litmus test needed to prove that this is a US State Department smokescreen—Saudi Arabia. Saudi Arabia, one of your closest Middle East allies, supports many different facets of international Islamist terrorism, covertly funding groups such as the Taliban and Al Qaeda. Of the 19 hijackers responsible for 9/11, 15 hailed from Saudi Arabia. Not one was from Iran. Yet why is Saudi Arabia mysteriously absent from the US State Department's list of 'State Sponsors of Terrorism' while Iran remains at the top year after year?

"Iran, and Venezuela as well, are being singled out not because of terrorism or communism, but because of a far more powerful '-ism' at work in the world today—globalism—which has become nothing more than a diplomatic disguise for US imperialism and unquestionably the most unstoppable force at work on the planet today.

"If advancing freedom and democracy were your nation's true motive, then surely the extremely repressive and authoritarian regimes of Saudi Arabia and Bahrain would be under major scrutiny right alongside Iran. But because they are willing to play the game and keep the oil concessions flowing, they are called friends and allies, while Iran remains in the crosshairs as public enemy number one.

"Yet the most ironic part of it all is one unavoidable truth—the United States needs Iran. The military machine needs an enemy to justify its massive expenditures. Politicians need a dog whistle to galvanize the vote. And people everywhere seem to need someone else to blame and to hate and to grind their teeth at. But Iranians are a truly beautiful people. You smile when I talk about the Persians—their exotic food, their towering and spiraling architecture, their exquisite rugs. But how many today even know that Iran *is* Persia? Persia simply got a name change in 1935 to Iran, which is nothing more than the name of the country in Persian. Yet how that name and that nation and its people have become poison on the lips of your people. Iranians are your brothers and sisters, Jim. So are Venezuelans. No different from you in any way. And until you and your people can see that, there is no hope for America—or for the world."

"I, I," Jim began but his voice sputtered out. He took a deep breath and swallowed hard. "I want to love. I want to love *them*. I want to love everyone."

"I know, Jim," Mosaddegh responded with a glimmer of heartfelt compassion in his eyes, "that's why the Great Spirit has chosen you. Listen close, you are about to be appointed as the United States Ambassador to the United Nations, an organization founded to assert the principle of self-determination into international law and diplomacy. What this means is that every nation in existence deserves the right to determine its own future and destiny.

"Yet your nation, as the very leader of this organization, seems dead-set on making sure that its heavy hand looms over all the rest. And if any inkling of dissent arises, retaliation comes swift and strong. The real story behind the crippling economic warfare being waged against Iran and Venezuela is a brand of self-determination that satirically is intolerable to the nation that hosts the international organization designed to uphold this very virtue around the globe. And a nation that proudly attributes its own existence to the exact same attribute. Remember the Boston Tea Party?

"Jim, the United States of America is not the invisible hand, and when you pretend to be, the consequences are devastating. You and the leaders of your nation must stop trying to hold on to everything so tightly and let the people of the world go from your crippling vice grip. Because whether or not you live long enough for it to backfire on you, it will most certainly backfire on your children and your children's children—unless something radically changes."

In a flash, the enormous lion disappeared in what felt like a whirlwind that sent a second gust of wind hurtling in Jim's direction. He stood with his back still to the wall as if frozen solid. He felt like days had passed but knew from experience that no more than a minute or two of natural time had most likely elapsed.

XIX

Jim took a long, deep breath and tried to regain both his senses and his composure. He swung around to the front of the mirror once again and examined his reflection. Aside from the ever-deepening wrinkles and the constantly multiplying gray hairs that he would never allow himself to get over, he looked no worse for the wear. He straightened up his back, adjusted his tie knot and patted his hair down before making his move toward the door.

Jim returned down the same spacious hallway to find the receptionist and Larry in the exact same positions as he had left them.

"Larry," Jim whispered after he had settled back down in his chair. "How long was I in the bathroom just now?"

"What kind of question is that?" asked Larry, shooting Jim a strange look. "You were gone three minutes. Are you feeling alright? You were looking a little queasy earlier."

"I'm fine," Jim said. "It's just nerves, that's all. This is a big deal, and it's just that, it's all so sudden, you know?"

"I know, Jim old boy," Larry reassured him. "Well, you don't have anything to worry about. You're in good hands now."

Jim and Larry resumed their mutual silence and both got to

work on their cell phones. Half an hour went by unnoticeably, and then the phone on the receptionist's desk rang.

"West Wing, this is Jennifer," she spoke into the receiver. "Yes. Yes, I will send him right up," she said after a brief pause and then hung up the handset.

"Jim, Jim Hamilton?" she said his name as a question.

"Yes, ma'am," Jim replied with a tinge of a Southern drawl.

"The Vice President will see you now, on the second floor. The President has a two o'clock departure on Marine One. He will try to see you before then if at all possible. Would you like a sandwich for lunch? It's getting close to noon. They make a mean Reuben."

"A Reuben would be great," Jim responded politely.

"Perfect. Just take a left at the end of the hall, and the elevator will be on your right. Once you get off on the second floor, take another left and look for the Office of Legislative Affairs. Do you have any questions?"

"I do," Larry piped up. "Y'all got a Reuben for me?"

"No, Mr. Wade. We do not. But it is always a pleasure to see you."

"That figures," Larry mumbled under his breath. "Alright, Jim. Looks like you're on your own."

With that, Larry gave him a brazen slap on the back with his left hand and extended his right to Jim like he was closing some kind of business deal.

"Thanks a lot, Larry," Jim said as he grasped Larry's outstretched hand. "I can't tell you how much I appreciate it. It's good to see you. You're looking well."

"Well like a middle-aged car salesman," Larry replied with a smirk. "Just trying to make it through the day and steer clear of the lemons."

Larry stood to his feet, and Jim immediately followed suit. "Jennifer, it's been a pleasure," Larry belted out. He then gave a lackluster military salute and was out the door.

Jim watched him go in a half-daze as if he was watching a caricature from a bad 80s sitcom, and suddenly he realized that he was on his own. He nodded to the receptionist and began his short trek down the hallway toward the elevator. The short wait in reception had helped Jim regain his bearings, but the nerves instantly returned as soon as Larry left.

Up to this point, Jim had pictured Larry being by his side throughout the process and had even imagined being able to turn to Larry if some tough question were to arise so that he could explain how all of this had been thrust upon Jim on such short notice and how he needed some time to take it all in. Now, everything seemed to rest squarely on his shoulders.

The short ride in the elevator seemed to take an eternity, and Jim experienced a sinking feeling in his stomach when the doors finally opened. He debated whether or not he should just stay on the elevator and let the doors close and go back down to the first floor and walk right past the receptionist and exit out of the front door never again to return. But something held him fast on his course, and he knew exactly what it was, that it was his destiny finding him out in an unfamiliar place and at a completely unexpected time.

He followed Jennifer's instructions and quickly found the

door labeled "Office of Legislative Affairs" slightly ajar, so he knocked lightly and gently pushed his way in. He was relieved to find the front partition of the office empty and breathed a small sigh of relief as he surveyed his surroundings. The walls were covered with built-in mahogany bookcases that housed row after row of massive, important-looking tomes that you usually only find in lawyer's offices and museums.

In the center of the room sat a large, round antique drum table which appeared to be made of Rosewood with four plush leather chairs surrounding it. On opposite sides of the table, two Reubens were plated on gold rimmed white china and served with potato chips and a pickle. Jim sauntered around the room pretending to look at the books and debating in his mind whether to sit at the table or to remain standing. Just as he was finishing his second lap and starting to feel a bit awkward, a head poked through the threshold of the open door.

"Please have a seat, Mr. Hamilton, and make yourself at home," the young man said briskly. "The Vice President will be with you shortly."

"Oh, thank you," Jim replied. "How did you know that—" he began to ask about the sandwich, but the young man had already disappeared from the doorframe. Jim stood with his mouth open for just a moment and then took a seat at one of the two places which had been set at the table. He pulled his chair in, removed the white linen napkin from under a well-polished silver fork, and placed the napkin squarely in his lap.

Then Jim waited. He waited and waited and waited. He didn't dare pull out his phone and risk getting caught by the second-incommand of the free world scrolling through his Twitter feed or something. He also did not dare eat the sandwich in front of him for fear of offending his host. So he sat and looked around the room and nervously picked at his fingernails as a string of subconscious prayers began to unwittingly form on his lips.

His prayers were not remotely eloquent and sounded a lot like pleas from a guilty man to his executioner. "Help me," Jim caught himself repeating as he attempted to draw steady, even breaths, followed by, "Have mercy," on the subsequent exhales. He did not even fully realize what he was doing until he would occasionally catch himself and suppress his reflexive mumblings. Then after a few minutes, he would inadvertently start back up again.

He thought about his life up to this point and reflected on all of the unpredictable twists and turns which had led him to this fateful moment in time. He felt that there must indeed be a god or a guiding force, an invisible hand of some sort, because coincidence was just not strong enough of a word. Perhaps, it was the Great Spirit, as Mosaddegh had suggested, although the idea still seemed so farfetched and far removed from his everyday life. Yet at the very same time, Jim felt as he looked back over his life that there was something with him all along, something that he could not quite put his finger on, something he only caught glimpses of in those rare moments of awe and spiritual clarity.

Due to the nature of the meeting at hand, Jim did not allow his mind to wander too far. He kept drawing his thoughts back to the present moment and rehearsing his first couple of lines to himself. As with the President, he had met the Vice President once at a campaign rally, but it had been years and the conversation had been brief and unmemorable.

After a long time had passed, Jim began to squirm in his chair a bit. The smell of the Reuben had tempted him at first, but he had managed to block it out for the most part. Now the aroma was beginning to wear on him, and it made his empty stomach gurgle. He pushed thoughts of bitterness and victimization out of his head and extended grace to his host who was, as he knew all too well, a busy man.

Just as he was entertaining the thought of standing up to stretch his legs, the same head and shoulders from before appeared in the doorway, only this time with a full body in view underneath them. The body contorted and assumed a painful-looking pose even before the head spoke, clasping both hands together and craning forward ever so slightly. Jim knew that the news could not be good.

"Mr. Hamilton," the young man began, "I am *so* sorry. Something has come up, and the Vice President regrettably has to cancel your meeting. Again, I am *very* sorry. He just had no other option. Is there anything I can *get* for you? Please feel free to eat your lunch. I hate that it got so cold."

Jim felt ice water rush down his spine as the one thought he refused to entertain during his ordeal of patience was coming to pass. Yet Jim knew this young fellow had nothing to do with anything. He was the only the messenger, and it never pays to kill the messenger.

"It's quite alright," Jim responded dully but still with an air of civility. "Hey, I meant to ask you. How did you know I ordered a Reuben?"

"Everyone gets the Reuben, Mr. Hamilton. Now if you will please pardon me, I must be going. It was a pleasure to meet you, sir."

And with that, the young man disappeared from the doorframe and flew off down the hall. Jim peered down at the cold sandwich, and for the first time since he had sat down in front of it, he found that he had absolutely no appetite. He slowly pushed away from the table, stretching his legs and back as he stood, and he poked his head out of the door to make sure that the coast was clear before stepping out into the hallway and heading back toward the elevator.

Jim did not say a word to Jennifer as he walked past her desk toward the front door. He simply did not have it in him. Instead, he gave her a nod and proceeded straight out the door to the paved driveway surrounding the North Lawn. He caught himself staring at the ground and then remembered the words of the great lion—yet he could not find the grace to pick his head up at that moment.

XX

Jim wound his way back through the two security check-points where he had entered the White House grounds and took a left onto Pennsylvania Ave, followed by another quick left onto 17th Street. Half a block away from the White House, he pulled out his phone and dialed Larry's number. The phone rang and rang, but he got no answer. Eventually, it connected him through to Larry's voicemail.

"Larry, this is Jim. I don't know what kind of sick joke that was, but I am done. I've wasted half of my day, I missed my committee meeting and the governor's lunch, and I'm going to have to tell Penny that the whole thing was a bust. If you get any more bright ideas, you can just keep them to yourself!"

As he ended the call, Jim found himself missing the good old days when you could make a real statement hanging up a telephone receiver. Pushing the little red button just wasn't enough of an outlet for a moment like this, and Jim was too frugal to throw his phone onto the sidewalk, although he seriously considered it.

He thrust his phone back into his pocket and began pacing the streets of the nation's capital for the second time that day. He fumed under his breath to himself, mostly dreading the embarrassment of facing Penny after making such a big to-do and pulling her aside earlier in the day.

Things had just been so tense with her that he tried at all costs to avoid making any sort of misstep, particularly since the backlash as of late had been so severe. He realized that he could not shift the blame for a single moment, but nonetheless, it stung deep and long like a slap in the face on a bitter cold day.

I should have known better than to trust Larry, Jim told himself as his long strides moved him along the sidewalk at a furious pace. *He always used to bite off more than he could chew, and I guess nothing has changed. I'll think twice before I rearrange my whole schedule for him again.*

Jim contemplated hailing a taxi and heading back to the Governors Association meeting for the afternoon, but what would he tell everyone? He eventually decided after some deliberation that it would be better just to miss the whole thing than to have to make up a story about why he missed half of the day. He gripped his hands tightly into fists as he continued on his tirade down 17th Street.

Suddenly, Jim stumbled over something, and as he looked back, he saw coins and dollar bills scattered all over the gray concrete like an explosion emanating out from a crumpled paper cup that lay on its side like a fallen soldier. Behind the newly created mess sat a small, grey-haired woman perched in a low beach chair with a bright umbrella overhead and a plethora of homemade signs positioned all around her.

"I'm so sorry," Jim exclaimed as he instinctively bent down to collect the loose change that lay strewn all about his feet.

"Why don't you watch where you're going?" the woman bellowed at almost exactly the same time. "And I don't need any help," she continued as she eased out of her chair to begin collecting quarters and nickels and dimes into her flattened cup, which she gently reshaped the best she could back into its original form.

"I just, I just didn't see you there," Jim said half to himself as he reached for a far-flung quarter which had rolled to the very edge of the sidewalk.

"Well, no, I guess not, the way you were walking," the woman replied, sounding slightly less startled. "You were pacing like a madman. You're just like the rest of them. Too busy to stop, too busy to say, 'hello'—too busy to even look where they're going."

Jim thought about the profound nature of her comment for a moment before responding. "Like I said, I'm really very sorry. It's just been a rough day, that's all. Here, I think this is the last one," he said as he handed her a dollar bill that he had stopped with his foot from floating away in the wind. "What's your name?"

"Suzanne," the woman replied in a much more even tone. "But everyone calls me Mami Suzy."

As she spoke, Jim began for the first time to read the signs that were displayed all around her small beach chair.

Love Not War. Bombs Kill. End War Before It Ends Us. Just Say No To Nukes. Then Jim saw a sign out of the corner of his eye that caught his attention—*Hands Off Venezuela.*

"Ma'am," he spoke gently as Suzy was still getting settled back into her chair. "Do you mind telling me about this one?" he asked, pointing to the sign.

"What do you care about Venezuela?" she said sharply as she turned her head to look him square in the eyes.

"It's kind of complicated," Jim replied. "Let's just say that I've recently developed a heart for the nation."

"Well, it's just terrible what we're doing down there," Suzy responded, slowly shaking her head back and forth. "The pictures can't capture it because it's an invisible war. Do you know what siege warfare is? That's all a sanction really is, you know, a war of attrition. You cut off all the supply routes and starve them into submission. Or at least see how long they can last without toilet paper before they give in and let us install our man—Geedado, or whatever his name is."

"Guaido," Jim asserted after a short pause.

"That's it," she exclaimed almost in a shout. "That's the one. I've seen him. He wouldn't last one day without his double-ply." With this, she exploded into a burst of laughter that caught Jim completely off guard.

Jim observed her for a moment until the laughter died down. "How can you laugh about a horrible situation like what's going on in Venezuela?" Jim asked somewhat skeptically.

"Honey," Suzy replied, fixing her gaze on him. "I've seen a lot with these eyes. And I learned long ago that if I don't laugh, I'll cry."

Jim was not sure how to respond, so he remained silent until she spoke again.

"I am an American," Suzy continued, "but I spent 30 years in Nicaragua running an orphanage. You just can't imagine these kids—you have never seen anything so precious in your whole life. We took in the ones we could, but there were always more, always more. So every week, we went from barrio to barrio feeding the children we couldn't house. They would line up with their bowls, and no matter what we fed them, whatever we could scrounge up to put in a soup for those beautiful souls, they would eat every last bite and thank us with all of their hearts. Try feeding fish head stew to a bunch of American kids, and you'll see what I mean."

Suzy threw her head back as hearty laughter once again spilled out of her being, as if there were a wellspring of joy somewhere deep inside of her. Jim stood awkwardly looking on and could feel his cheeks turning red at the sight, not quite sure what to do with his hands or his posture in response to her vigorous movements and overt display of emotion. He started to put his hands into his pockets but immediately felt stiff, so he eventually crouched down beside her and put one knee to the pavement as he propped his hands on the other.

"Well, that's much better," Suzy said with a nod, "not hovering over me like most folks do, what did you say your name was?"

"Jim," he answered. "Jim Hamilton."

"It's a pleasure, Jim Hamilton," Suzy responded as she reached out her hand daintily. Jim put his hand into hers and gave it a little squeeze before letting go. "And where are you off to in such a big hurry?" she asked, gesturing toward the busy sidewalk that continued to bustle with foot traffic right beside them.

"Oh, nowhere really. It's just, I was more running *away* from something than going *to* something. I feel like that's the story of my life sometimes." Jim let out a sigh and began to rub his chin as he did when he found himself deep in thought. "But please, tell me more about your orphanage, in Nicaragua did you say?"

"Yes, good old Nica," Suzy said as a nostalgic smile slowly widened across her face. "The orphanage was beautiful. We never had enough money, but we always had love. And God was on our side. God is always on your side when you fight for people. And that's what we did. We fought for the people. For the children, for their parents, for anyone and everyone we met along the way. I'm a fighter you see. I may not be big, but don't let size fool you. Big things come in small packages."

Jim knew Suzy was finished speaking because she burst forth into yet another round of wild laughter. This time it tickled him, and he couldn't help but to start chuckling right alongside her. After a moment, he began again with another question.

"If it was so good," Jim asked thoughtfully, "what made you come back to the states?"

"Who said anything about it being good?" she replied rather sharply, furrowing her brow at him. "It's miserable down there. The children are precious, beyond precious, but the government is so corrupt. You can't win in Latin America. Not in Nicaragua, not in Guatemala, not anywhere. Hey, it's America's backyard, right? So what you end up getting is an iron fisted, US-backed puppet or a reactionary socialist revolutionary. There is no in between—and it's hard to tell which is worse.

"You know," Suzy continued, "we house the kids and feed them, we clothe them and, and we truly love them. But then they grow up and they go to the government to get a business license and they have to pay this fee and bribe that official, and by the time it's all said and done, they can't make an honest buck. You can only give people handouts for so long before they become completely dependent—sort of institutionalized. Eventually if you don't give them something to do, some responsibility or a job where they can use their hands and their God-given gifts and talents to improve the world around them, well, there's just nothing you can do for that individual after a while.

"So I moved back to the states because there was nothing left for me to do on the ground level there. The real changes need to happen here, in this city, in our halls of power—and not just for Nica. It's worse than you can imagine out there, all these poor nations under US scrutiny and control. Someone needs to tell these hawks to take their hands off the rest of the world. And don't for a second believe it's Republicans versus Democrats. War and global military dominance are perhaps the only bipartisan point of convergence in our whole political system. Watch them bicker over bathrooms and drinking straws and who to indict next, but see how few of them will ever raise their voice against the war machine. It's a real racket, you know."

"Why do you think that is?" Jim asked solemnly.

"Oh, it's very simple," Suzy started to explain. "In order to run for office, politicians need corporate sponsorships. And for corporations to thrive in a global economy, they need military protection. It would be against corporate self-interest to back anti-war candidates. War is extremely profitable. Corporations get contracts to build weapons, to blow stuff up and then to rebuild what they destroyed. Not to mention contracts to feed, clothe, and take care of millions of soldiers and civilians doing the work on the ground.

"The rest of the corporate world then benefits from the constant pressure put on other countries by our State Department to align with our economic interests and to create favorable conditions for our corporate presence. When Apple or Berkshire Hathaway walk into a board room in any country around the world, it's not just a bunch of business execs showing up in expensive suits. They have a lot of firepower behind them, and everyone in the room is perfectly aware.

"Until we get some kind of campaign finance reform going, which the majority of average Americans are in favor of, the agenda of our politicians will continue to conform to that of the corporations who front the money to put them in office. Otherwise, we're pretty stuck. I would run for office myself, but they say I have a face for radio."

Suzy's eyes twinkled as she belted out another round of raucous laughter. Jim couldn't help but laugh right along with her despite an internal tug of resistance due to the serious nature of the conversation at hand. He looked at her in amazement and recognized something in her that he had only seen in one other person in his entire life—his Great Aunt Edith, who had taught elementary school in the inner city of Chicago for nearly half a century.

"Pardon me for asking," Jim began cautiously, "but how did you get like this? I mean, so full of joy, yet so determined at the same time?"

Suzy shrugged her shoulders and shook her head slowly as she averted her gaze to the gray concrete beneath her. Jim could see small tear drops forming in her eyes just before she wiped them away with her coat sleeve. She took a deep breath and lifted her eyes to his once again.

"When I was a little girl, I had a twin sister who was the world to me. We played together, we sang together—we did everything together. When we were 10 years old, she had a horseback riding accident and became paralyzed from the neck down. She died of complications two years later. I was so mad at God. I couldn't eat. I couldn't go to school. I just sat in my room and cried. For two whole months.

"Then one night, a man in white appeared to me. He walked across the room and sat next to me on my bed. He stared deeply into my eyes, and do you know what I saw there? Fire. Flickering flames of fire. Not fire that was about to die out, but fire that was about to roar up and consume my entire being. I didn't notice it right away, but as we sat there, all of my sadness melted away and I felt perfect peace. I thought he must be an angel. Then he spoke. He told me that my sister was alright, that she was with God. Then he disappeared."

Suzy choked back sobs as she attempted to keep her composure. "After that day, I gave my life to God and asked him to use me however he wanted. But as I grew older, it upset me to see the apathy and hypocrisy of those who called themselves followers of God, so I went to Nicaragua to see if I could find something different. And boy did I ever.

"There was so much pain, so much poverty, but it was the children who changed me. Their piercing eyes asked the same question every time I would look into them—are you going to show me God or just talk about him? So I wept and I prayed until the day God gave me the land for the orphanage. There are more than 200 children living there right now as we speak. I long to go back, every day I do, but this is my assignment for this season. And to be honest, I'm not even sure why quite yet."

Jim could hardly contain himself as Suzy finished her story.

"It's me!" he exclaimed. "I mean, I don't want to, I don't mean to be arrogant. But I believe you're here—for me. Do you know who I am?"

Suzy blinked twice. "You're Jim Hamilton," she said flatly.

"Yes, Jim Hamilton, the governor of Georgia who just walked here from a meeting with the Vice President at the White House. Well, it got canceled, but I am supposed to be meeting with the President himself this weekend, and I, I don't know what on earth I'm going to tell him. But if you could just come with me, then you could share with him your experiences and all that you just told me. You could have your platform. The whole world needs to hear what you have to say, Suzy."

Suzy closed her eyes, and a sullen look moved across her face. For a moment, Jim was puzzled. Then he realized that she was praying. He waited quietly for several moments as his heart continued to beat rapidly in his chest.

At last, Suzy opened her eyes and smiled a radiant smile as bright and beautiful as any he had ever seen in his life. "My child," she began softly yet sternly, "I cannot go with you. Everything you need is already inside of you. The only weapon you need for this battle is love. Don't focus on what you don't know. Just focus on what you do. The children need you, Jim. You don't know them—yet—but I can see your love for them. They deserve a chance. And you're going to give it to them."

With that, Suzy closed her eyes again and buried her face in her hands. Jim wanted to comfort her, but at that moment, his phone began to vibrate in his pocket. Something told him to look at it, so he pulled it out and saw that Larry was returning his call.

Jim rose to his feet as quietly as he could and answered the call, whispering into the receiver as he tiptoed away from Suzy. "Larry, what's going on?"

"Jim!" Larry sounded frantic. "Are you nuts? I leave you alone for one hour and you disappear on me. The Vice President had a family emergency and is on his way to Indiana as we speak. That doesn't mean you storm out of the place! The President is leaving in 45 minutes from the South Lawn on Marine One. He still wants to meet with you. How quickly can you get your tail back over here?"

"Relax, Larry," Jim said with a strange coolness in his voice. "I'm right around the corner on 17th. I can be there in five minutes."

"Ok, good," Larry's voice came back, followed by a long sigh. "Meet me at the first security checkpoint on the north side, and I will get you back in. For God's sake, Jim, you almost gave me a heart attack there."

"Ten-four, Larry," Jim responded as he ended the call.

He returned the phone to his pocket and raced back to Suzy's chair, where he found her sitting in the exact same position she had been in when he first stumbled over her change cup.

"Suzy, I have to go," Jim puffed, nearly out of breath from sheer excitement. "How can I get in touch with you? Here take this." He pulled out all of the cash from his wallet, folded it and squeezed it into her hand.

"Keep your filthy lucre," she said, pulling her hand away and placing it firmly over his heart. "But never lose this."

Jim closed his eyes and took a deep breath before opening

them again. "Thank you," he said quietly and with great sincerity. "I will come back and let you know how it goes."

"Oh, I already know how it's going to go, dear," Suzy replied, beaming with an exuberant grin. "Now run along—your destiny awaits you."

Jim held out the cash to her one last time, looking a little bit like a guilty puppy, and Suzy gently shook her head, still grinning from ear to ear. After a brief pause, he shoved the money into his pocket and took off back down 17th Street. If his pace had been a frantic walk before, then his current stride was closer to a full-on run. He was very careful to watch his feet and had to slow down a couple of times where the pedestrian traffic on the sidewalk grew heavy. But still, he managed to beat Larry to the checkpoint, who sauntered up two minutes after Jim had arrived.

"You ready?" Larry shouted when we was still about 10 yards out.

"It's now or never," Jim echoed back. They shook hands, and Larry pulled out his security badge, motioning for Jim to approach the checkpoint. After clearing both security lines, they walked up the same driveway to the West Wing as before. They entered through the front door and greeted Jennifer, who was still sitting at her desk. Jim found himself utterly embarrassed to face her and began to blush before he even reached her desk.

"Hello, gentlemen," Jennifer said, raising her eyebrows slightly. "You're back."

"Yeah, yeah," Larry cut in. "What's the update?"

"The President will meet you on the Oval Office Patio before his two o'clock flight. You are just in time. I will let him know you're here."

Jennifer picked up the receiver on her desk and began to dial a number. "Mr. Wade, you will escort our guest won't you?"

"On our way," Larry said as he waved for Jim to follow him. He led them down a series of winding hallways until Jim was completely turned around. Finally, Larry opened a door that led them back outside onto a large slate patio, which was partially covered by a large white arbor and decorated with a handful of black wrought iron tables and chairs. Tiny white blossoms spotted the confederate jasmine vines hanging over the sides and down through the top latticework of the wooden arbor as yellow and red tulips brightened the ground all around.

Larry motioned for Jim to have a seat. "You're not going to have to wait as long as you did last time, Jim old boy. There's Marine One now."

Jim looked up and peered through the trees to the South Lawn where he could see the Presidential helicopter parked not more than 100 yards away.

"I hope not," Jim said mostly to himself. "Those Reubens belonged in a museum once we were done."

"What's that?" Larry asked, holding his hand to his ear.

"Oh, nothing. Say, what I am expected to do here, anyway? Is this like a meeting of the minds over foreign policy or just a formality?"

"Somewhere between the two, but definitely leaning toward the formality side. You just want to tell him what an honor it is to be selected for the position and that you look forward to serving and all that jazz. You know the deal, Jim. Just please, don't come out with anything from left field, alright?"

"Ok, ok. I've got it," Jim replied. "If we even get to meet with him."

"Listen, you've got to lighten up, Jim," Larry fired back tersely. "Things happen. You know better than any. Look, here we go now." As he spoke, Larry gestured to a man in a black suit with a very serious look on his face walking briskly toward them. He spoke into an earpiece microphone as he walked, and his pace was so intent that his whole body seemed to lean forward at an angle like a listing sailboat.

The man walked right up to Jim without even so much as acknowledging Larry and spoke briskly. "Mr. Hamilton," he said rather mechanically, "the President is honored to have you at the White House today. He will meet with you now. Will you please follow me?"

Jim looked over at Larry flat-lipped and nodded to the man. "Yes," he said. "And it's an honor to be here."

The Secret Service Agent turned on a dime like a tin soldier and began walking in the same direction from which he came. Jim and Larry immediately fell in line behind him, following him out of the patio, alongside the Rose Garden and across to the top of the South Lawn, where he finally came to a halt with Marine One behind him and the White House in front. As quickly as he had appeared, the agent was gone, disappearing into the south entrance of the White House, as two more agents took posts on either side of Jim. Larry stood a couple of paces away and suddenly looked more like a bystander than a primary actor.

It all happened so fast. The President and two of his aides exploded from the White House doors surrounded by about half a dozen agents all dressed exactly the same as the first three. The President waved to Jim, who began to take a step forward, but the agent to his left held out his arm, motioning for Jim to stay put. Jim waited stiffly until the President's entourage finally met him.

"Jim Hamilton," the President belted out confidently as he extended his right hand. "You look even better than you did when I last saw you back in 2016."

Jim tried with all of his might to maintain his poise as he clasped the outstretched hand of the President of the United States of America. "You haven't aged a day yourself," Jim shot back, matching the President's tone. "Thank you for having me."

"We only have a minute, Jim," the President began again, "but this is really just a formality. I wanted to lay my eyes on you and ask you in person, since you were already in town, if you would serve as my Ambassador to the United Nations. I know the kind of stuff you're made of, Jim, and I believe you're the man for the job."

"It would be an absolute honor, sir," Jim responded, surprising himself a little with the crisp and bold quality of his own voice. It reminded him of the old days, before his fall from public grace.

"Listen," the President continued, "we have a lot to discuss.

I'll get you up here once we're back from Camp David, toward the end of next week. For now—"

As quick as lightning, Jim saw a glimmer of metal out of the corner of his eye and lunged at the President half a second before the gun discharged twice, lodging two bullets in Jim's lower abdomen. Immediately, the aide who had fired the shots was wrestled to the ground and could barely be seen beneath the pile of Secret Service Agents covering him.

Jim felt no pain at first. The adrenaline numbed everything except his racing mind, which kept repeating the same question over and over again. *Did I just tackle the President of the United States of America?*

Yet as Jim lay on the cool grass, reality began to sink in and a surge of pain crashed over his body like a tidal wave of unparalleled magnitude. He looked down at his hands, which were ferociously gripping his stomach, and he could see the blood pouring over them and under them and even flowing out from between his fingers.

His body grew hot and then cold as the blood continued to flow from the bullet wounds, running down his sides and staining the grass beneath him. He thought about his mother and the way she used to hold him tight in her arms when his father would go off on his tirades and the incredible depth of comfort that it always brought him. He longed for her embrace now but knew that not even her touch could ease the pain he felt at this moment.

Suddenly, he sensed an arm slip underneath his head and felt his neck being lifted off the ground ever so slightly. Then he saw the face of the President only two feet in front of his. "Jim! Jim!" The President was shouting but his voice sounded like a muffled whisper, the entire scene unfolding as if in slow motion. He could see the agents running this way and that, more than he could ever have counted, their faces reflecting the flashing blue lights of the police cars that were racing up in droves. The sirens blared and the lights pulsed, and he could not tell if he was awake or asleep. Then instantly, Jim's whole world flashed back into real time, and the booming voice of the President and the sirens and the commotion hit his ears like a roaring freight train.

"Jim! Jim! Speak to me!" the President continued shouting. "Jim, you saved my life!"

Jim swallowed hard and fought to maintain consciousness.

"Jim, the stretcher is on its way," the President said, lowering his voice slightly. "Just hold on a little longer."

Jim lay motionless in the grass as he stared up into the face of the President. Then a thought popped into his mind, the thought that this might be his last waking moment on earth, his last chance to communicate all of the revelation he had received over the past three months. Despite the pain, Jim grit his teeth and determined not to let it pass in vain.

"Mr. President, Mr. President," Jim eked out between gasps of breath, "there is something I have to tell you."

"Jim, anything. What is it?"

"Iran. And Venezuela. We have to stop. The sanctions. The children are, we have to give this next generation a chance. Please, listen. You are the only one who can—"

At that moment, the President was jerked away by a handful of agents, and Jim could feel new bodies pressing in all around him as he was lifted onto a stretcher and frantically wheeled to the back of an ambulance which had sped into the circular drive.

Jim's eyes were closed, but he could tell when they moved him into the ambulance as the brightness of the daylight faded to darkness. He tried to open his eyes in order to survey his new surroundings, but his eyelids felt like lead and would not open at first. He eventually managed to open them just enough to see three EMTs working frantically all around him with tubes and gauze and very serious looks on their faces.

Jim closed his eyes once more and could feel his body becoming lighter and lighter, like it was floating upward through the roof of the ambulance and into the cool afternoon air. Suddenly, everything around him grew dazzling white, and Jim could feel a surge of warmth come over his entire body, expelling the chill that kept trying to enshroud him. The sense of weightlessness instantly became paired with a familiar sense of timelessness which made him think of his first encounter with Tatanka.

He could open his eyes effortlessly now, and when he did, he could not believe the sight that lay before him. A wide river sparkled and danced in the rays of the sun, winding its way through a vast expanse of trees and flowers which exploded with colors unlike any he had ever seen. The river seemed to run for miles and miles, until it reached a glimmering city pulsing with radiant brightness and splendor. As soon as he set eyes on it, he found himself in the middle of the city standing before a brilliant light which was impossible to look at and even more impossible to look away from. He felt a strange aura all around him as if he were surrounded by a vast throng of people, yet he could see nothing aside from the overpowering light in all directions.

As he stood entranced, he began to make out the faint outline of a figure in the very center of the light which slowly came into focus. As he watched the form take shape, he realized that it was Tatanka, the great bison. Yet before he could open his mouth, the silhouette began to shift and gradually took on the form of a large eagle. He remembered Freedom and wanted to call its name, but his lips were frozen and his tongue heavy. Next, the image of the eagle shifted into the outline of a smaller bird and then to an even smaller bird, which Jim recognized respectively as Jim Crow and the troupial, Bolívar.

The figure then grew and grew into the form of the mighty carabao, Aguinaldo, and finally the majestic lion, Mossaddegh, who gradually came into full clarity right before his eyes. The Asiatic lion approached him swishing its tail back and forth, its mane gently swaying and its eyes laser locked onto his. But then a fascinating thing happened. The face of the lion slowly began to morph and change into the face of a man, its flowing mane turning into wild locks of curly dark hair right before his eyes. Its nose and ears and mouth all transformed in similar fashion—only the eyes remained, eyes of burning fire which seemed to pierce his soul.

Suddenly, Jim could feel his lips and his tongue begin to

loosen, and he knew in that moment that he could speak again. He gathered his courage, for it was a beautiful place yet dreadful at the same time, and he spoke to the man who was now standing fully upright before him.

"Who are you?" Jim said in the boldest voice he could muster, although the sound emerged from his vocal chords like nothing more than the peep of a mouse in that great cavernous place.

"I am God, your Creator," the being replied in a voice which reverberated with the power of a roaring river or a booming clap of thunder, yet that carried the melodic quality of an angelic choir.

Jim stood silent in awe of the voice, which not only resonated deep within the core of his being, but that also enveloped him with a feeling of soothing warmth and unconditional love.

"You were expecting to speak with Tatanka or Mosaddegh were you, Jim? Or the Great Spirit even? Are you surprised to discover that *I am* behind them all?"

"But, but how? How could you be, and why, why did you take on all of those different forms?"

"I appeared to you as you were able and willing to receive me. Because of your past, I could not reveal myself to you in this way. Not initially. You carried far too much baggage. You thought that you knew all about me then, so you would have projected the image you had in your mind onto me. I could never have reached you that way. But now that you have encountered these different facets of my being, you can begin to see my true nature."

Jim's mind reeled and raced as he grappled with this new revelation. He took a deep breath and remained silent.

"I love you more than you could ever know, Jim. And I have been with you every step of your life's journey, both when you sought me and when you couldn't care less about me. You have misunderstood me from your earliest days. But I am not who you think I am. I am the God of justice. And the God of peace. I fight for the hurting and for the poor, and I make wars cease to the ends of the earth. I am not done with you yet, Jim. You must go back. You have a purpose to fulfill on the earth, to be a peacemaker in my name. But before you go, I must show you the depth of my love."

As soon as these words reached Jim's ears, he could feel himself being lifted up and whisked away to a dark hillside. The ground was rocky underneath his feet, and he sensed a cold chill move across his entire body, much like the coldness that had tried to creep over him just before he was taken away in the ambulance.

Something inside told him to look up, and what he saw before his eyes was nearly unrecognizable. About 50 feet in front of him hung the mangled form of a human body covered from head to toe in open wounds and dripping with blood. The figure was muttering something over and over again that he could not make out at his current distance.

Jim found his footing and began to walk toward the man, and in what felt like an instant, he found himself standing right beneath the horrible, bloody mess. The body was elevated, much higher than he had originally perceived, and as he looked up, he noticed two wooden beams in the shape of a cross behind the man, supporting his weight.

Large metal spikes had been driven through both hands and both feet, holding them firmly in place, and a crown of thorns had been pressed down onto his brow, causing a constant trickle of blood to drip down over his eyes and face. Jim could just begin to make out the words that this tortured person was repeating over and over again. "Father, forgive them, for they know not what they do."

Jim fell to his knees as a mixture of sickness and sorrow overwhelmed him, and he began to sob uncontrollably. He felt that he couldn't stand the blood and the gore and the stench of death any longer, and he wished that it would all just go away. At that very moment, he felt the light and the warmth return all around him, and he heard a voice from behind him saying, "This, Jim, is my love for you—the cross that I endured for you."

Jim stood to his feet and spun around, and there before him was the same radiant image of the man who had spoken to him before.

"I am Jesus," the resplendent man continued, "the Son of God and the Savior of the world. On that bloody cross, I paid the price for all of the evil and all of the wars and all of the death that has plagued the earth since the beginning of human history. I died, but death could not hold me, and now I am alive forever more. I have been grossly misrepresented in every age since my coming. People have wrongly taken my gospel and made it all about great buildings and grand services. They have used my name to gain wealth and honor, prestige and power. They have made my message about rules and restrictions rather than love and compassion, what not to do rather than my heart to fight for the very least on this planet. But they are in for a rude awakening. I came to love people, not to cast stones at them. I love everyone and forgive all who come to me. I am the defender of the poor and the needy, not the rich and the power-ful. I fight for the least and I would know—I became the very least so that all could become great. In my name. Through the power of my love.

"I am going to use you, Jim. To fight for the nameless, face-less victims of war and oppression all over the precious earth that I created. But first, you had to see my love. You had to know the depths of sorrow and suffering that I was willing to endure to save my children. And you had to know my name. This is only a glimpse, Jim. My love is greater than you will ever know. Now you must go back and finish your work on the earth. Do I have your allegiance?"

"My allegiance?" Jim asked, raising his eyebrows.

"Your allegiance. To me and to my kingdom. To my love for humanity. To my purposes on the earth. There are many today who are trying to solve man's problems, but they are doing it man's way. You can't fight fire with fire. If mankind were able to solve its own problems, surely you would have done it by now. That's why I came, Jim. If it wasn't necessary for me to die on that horrible cross, I wouldn't have done it. If there was any other way for people to be forgiven for their wrongdoings and to enter my eternal kingdom, I would never have come to earth in the first place. But your sin problem had to be dealt with once and for all. Just think about it. If God allowed one thief into heaven, would your belongings ever be safe? If he let one murderer into heaven, would you ever be able to lie down in peace?

"God wants all of his children to enter heaven, but only those who repent of their sins and chose to be washed in my blood will be able to live with us in paradise. Otherwise, heaven simply wouldn't be heaven. God loves every single person on the planet exactly the same—but if someone refuses to let go of their sin, he can't allow them to enter and destroy the sanctity of his perfect home. All it takes is one naked child running around to ruin a wedding. If the child is given the proper clothes and refuses to put them on, then that is his choice. But he can't be allowed to spoil the entire ceremony for the sake of stubborn disobedience. Hell is not a place where God wants to send any of his children. Far from it. It's simply an alternative for those who refuse to be born again into the new nature of God's heavenly realm."

"Lord, I believe," Jim broke in, falling again to his knees. "Forgive me."

"I will and I have. You are forgiven because you have asked with a sincere heart. That's all it takes, Jim. Now, I can begin to use you, but you must be willing to follow me wherever I go, even to the death. You are not saved by turning to me once. You are saved by continuing to turn to me every day for the rest of your life. Are you ready to die to yourself—to your dreams, to your ambitions, to your idea of success—and live for me?"

"Well," Jim began slowly after a moment of contemplation, "I think I'm already dead. But yes, I am ready. What do I have left to lose?"

"You'll find out very soon. But I will always be with you, never forget that. I love you, Jim. Until we meet again."

Suddenly, the light and the peace that surrounded him fled, and Jim could feel cold, metal plates pressing hard against his chest. "Clear!" Shock waves pulsed through his body, and he gasped for breath, his chest arching to the ceiling. "He's breathing! I have a pulse. His heart rate is climbing. *Jim, Jim,* can you hear me?" Jim tried with all of his might to respond, but there was no strength left in his body. He finally gave in to the exhaustion, and his whole world went dark.

A peaceful sleep came over him, and the comfortable warmth returned all around him as his mind was filled with a dream of Suzy, his friend from 17th Street. In the dream, she was a child no more than 10 years old running through a field of red and yellow poppies, laughing and spinning and gliding her hands over the tops of the tall flowers.

Suddenly, another little girl appeared, and Suzy's eyes filled with tears as she sprinted to the girl and embraced her and smothered her with hugs and kisses, and somehow in his heart, Jim knew that it was her twin sister. After the wild jumble of arms and legs finally untangled, Jim could see the two girls running through the field together, flying white and gold ribbons and skipping through the flowers and laughing furiously— and the sound of that laughter was like heavenly music to his ears.

XXI

When Jim awoke, he could not tell by the analogue clock on the wall if it was three in the morning or three in the afternoon. Instantly, a surge of pain raced up from his gut, and he could feel the heaviness of his fatigued body as it pressed down onto the crisp white sheets of the hospital bed. He let out a low moan and froze his whole body, realizing that even the most miniscule movements caused discomfort from the bullet wounds.

"He's awake, he's awake," he heard a voice say from somewhere behind him. "Sounds like he's in pain. Someone call the nurse." He saw the silhouette of his daughter fly past his bed and out of the room in search of assistance. A moment later, his wife's face came into view as she gently peered over the edge of the bed.

"Well, hello, Mr. hero," she said in the softest tone he had heard from her in as long as he could remember.

"What, what day is it?" Jim asked groggily. "Did I die?"

Penny laughed out loud and then promptly covered her mouth. "Yes, Jim. You did die. For six minutes. But they brought you back. And today is Tuesday. You have been in a coma for three days."

Jim's head spun trying to grapple with this information. He felt like Rumpelstiltskin waking from a century-long nap. How could it have only been three days?

Before he had a chance to speak, Penny disappeared and came back to his bedside with something in her hands.

"Take a look at this," she began excitedly. "Can you read it, Jim?"

Jim tried to focus his eyes and could see from the header that she was holding up a copy of the Washington Post, but everything else looked like one big jumble of pictures and words and he could not get his mind in gear to focus on any one spot.

"Right there, Jim," she said patiently, pointing to a headline on the far right-hand side of the paper. "Here, let me read it to you. 'President Ends Decades of Sanctions Against Iran and Venezuela.' And another one just beneath it, 'Jim Hamilton Survives Shooting, Remains Unconscious at George Washington University Hospital.'"

"You're a hero, Jim," Penny continued. "You sure know how to start a new position with a bang. You are the first UN Ambassador to create a major foreign policy shift while in a coma. They are talking about ending dozens more, sanctions that is. Whatever you said to the President really made an impact. He came by and visited the day after you arrived."

"You mean," Jim said slowly, "that it wasn't a dream. That it all really happened. I, I really tackled the President?"

"You really tackled the President. Yes, Jim. And you took two bullets for him. Probably saved his life. One of his aides had some kind of vendetta against him. Said they had a bad run in a decade ago at one of his hotels, and he could never let it go. They still haven't released all of the details yet."

Jim closed his eyes as he attempted to process everything Penny had just told him, and as soon as he did, an image popped into his mind of Suzy sitting in her little beach chair with her umbrella overhead and surrounded by her protest signs. "I have to let her know," he said intently. "I have to let her know that God used her. And that she was right. It *was* her assignment."

"What are you talking about, Jim," Penny responded quizzically, gently placing her hand on her husband's forehead. "The only thing you have to do is to rest."

"Yes, yes. *Rest*." Jim relaxed his body and nestled his head back down into his pillow as he spoke. "Thank you, Penny. Thank you for being here. You are the only woman on the planet who would still be here. After all this. Thank you for not leaving. It's all going to be different now. You'll see. I'm a changed man." He smiled as the words left his mouth, having uttered that exact phrase countless times in the past.

"But talk is cheap," Jim added. "I'm going to show you that I mean it. One day at a time, my love. One day at a time."

XXII

Two days later, the phone rang in Jim's hospital room.

Jim could feel the stitches in his abdomen as he reached for the phone that sat on his bedside tray. "Hello?"

"Jim, it's Larry. I did what you said. I took a left onto 17th from Pennsylvania Ave and walked up and down for half a mile. There is no lady and no chair and no signs anywhere. She must have moved to a new location. I'm sorry, Jim. I gave it my best shot."

"Thanks, Larry," Jim said with a sigh. "I really appreciate it. Hey, one more thing. Why don't you ever call me on my cell phone? How'd you even get this number anyway?

"I have my ways, Jim. You just get some rest, and I'll come see you in a couple of days. Might even bring you some flowers if you're lucky."

"You couldn't fit another flower in this room if you tried," Jim joked. "Thanks again, old friend. I'll be seeing you."

"Whether you like it or not," Larry said with a chuckle.

Jim began to laugh but felt a sharp pain in his side, so he caught himself and carefully put the phone back on the tray. Jim could still remember the dream as vividly as if he had just woken up, of Suzy and her twin running and playing in that poppy field. He longed to know what had happened to her and to tell her all that had taken place since their fateful meeting.

Jim shifted his weight in the bed to find a more comfortable position and began to pray almost subconsciously under his breath. He asked God to bless Suzy, wherever she was. And to let her know that one life can make all the difference, no matter how small or insignificant in the eyes of the world, as long as that life is lived out in love.

Suddenly, a roll of laughter came over him that he could not quell, yet strangely he didn't feel a tinge of pain. He laughed that he was still alive, that Penny was by his side, that he was in this hospital room that never stopped beeping—and most of all that he was praying.

As his laughter died down, Jim spotted something out of the corner of his eye that had somehow evaded his notice up to this point.

"Penny," he called in a perplexed voice. "Penny, are you busy? Can I ask you something?"

"Yes, Jim," she responded from across the room. "What is it?"

"That hat," he said, pointing to a bright red *Make America Great Again* hat propped up in the windowsill against a vase of yellow daffodils. "Where did it come from?"

"One of the President's agents left it there for you," Penny answered. "Said it would mean something to you. It's been there since Sunday."

"Thanks, dear," Jim replied, his eyes fixed on the hat as Tatanka's mandate came crashing back into his mind—to make America great, not again, but for the first time, in a completely different way, not measured by GDP or by global economic dominance, but according to the Law of Love.

What an opportunity we have, Jim thought hopefully, *to show true greatness to the world. To protect the weak, to promote democracy, to cultivate freedom, to live up to our creeds. And to show the world what love looks like in action.*

A smile crept over Jim's face as he envisioned the compass rose and the old, tarnished globe that he saw in his first visit with Tatanka, the arrows stretching in every direction and wrapping all the way around the world from one end to the other—only this time they were not arrows of conquest, but arrows of love flying forth to the ends of the earth.

Instantly, a new vision flashed through his mind. He saw young men and women storming the nations of the earth carrying food rather than guns, planes flying over impoverished regions dropping medical supplies instead of bombs, diplomats at the table listening rather than speaking, and politicians publicly acknowledging the injustices of the past—determining never again to repeat them and committing to do all in their power to set things right.

Then Jim heard a still, small voice rising up from the depths of his heart. *Jim, now is the time to use your influence for good and not for greed, your technology for life and not for death, your resources for the poor of this world and not for the already wealthy. You have one chance to map a course never before seen in the history of the world—to use the power and reach of global empire to improve the lives of billions of people. It's now or never, Jim. This is your moment. America's moment. Make it count. The world is counting on you.*

Jim closed his eyes as tears began to stream down his cheeks. He sat motionless for a long time until the torrent of salty tears began to subside and eventually dry up altogether.

"I will," Jim whispered aloud. "But you have to help me."

"Who has to help you, Jim?" Penny's voice echoed from across the room.

"No one, dear," Jim said, wiping the tears from his eyes with the back of his hand. "I was just praying."

"You—were praying?" Penny asked skeptically.

"Yes, dear," Jim answered.

"Well, I never thought I'd see the day," Penny marveled half to herself.

"Me neither," Jim chuckled as he shifted his weight in the bed. "Me neither."

With a smile still on his face, Jim yawned deeply, closed his eyes once again, and drifted off to sleep.

CPSIA information can be obtained
at www.ICGtesting.com
Printed in the USA
LVHW022255280920
667360LV00002B/408

9 780985 412760